Bob Moats

I0567057

Bridezilla Murders

By Bob Moats

Copyright © 2009-2014 by Bob Moats

New Edits as of Sept, 2012

REV-0326141630

Bridezilla Murders

This book is licensed for your personal use only. This book may not be re-sold or given away to other people. If you would like to share this book with another person, please purchase an additional copy for each recipient. If you're reading this book and did not purchase it, or it was not purchased for your use only, please purchase your own copy. Thank you for respecting the hard work of this author.

No part of this book may be reproduced, scanned, or distributed in any printed or electronic form without permission. Please do not participate in or encourage piracy of copyrighted materials in violation of the author's rights. Purchase only authorized editions.

This is a work of pure fiction. Names, characters, places, and incidents either are the product of the author's imagination or are used fictitiously, and any resemblance to actual persons, living or dead, business establishments, events, or locales is entirely coincidental.

ISBN – 978-0-9960634-8-7

For information and address:
Magic 1 Productions
P.O. Box 524, Fraser MI 48026-0524
Website: http://murdernovels.com
Cover design by Bob Moats
Photo by Bob Moats

Bob Moats

Other Jim Richards series books by Bob Moats

For a preview or to purchase a book, go to
http://murdernovels.com

What a few people are saying about Murder Novels by Bob Moats

Mr. Moats, I just got your novel "Classmate Murders" and have to let you know, I read it in one evening. That is the first book I have ever done that with. That was the most enjoyable book I have ever read. I just started reading e-books, and reading again, after getting my wife a Kindle. This book was my 12th, and the best. I just got Las Vegas Showgirls to (read) tomorrow evening. I look forward to reading many of your books in this series. I have been searching for an author and books that were fun, entertaining reads. Your books are just the ticket.

Regards, A new fan, Bill from South Carolina

****

Another very nice comment submitted through my website from Micki P.:

"I recently was given a kindle for my 60th birthday. The first book I downloaded was the Classmate Murders and have now read every one of the them. Today I started on the Fatal Rejection series. Thank you for the wonderful ride with Jim and Penny and all the rest of the troop. I have laughed and giggled thru the stories, my poor family gave me the strangest looks! Now I really want a little Yorkie!! Fatal Rejection so far is another great read! I will be looking out for more of Jim Richards and since you are my #1 Author, anything of yours I can find."

Special thanks to:

To my new editor Sally Berneathy who under took the task of going through the most recent copy of this book and giving it the edits it has been needing. Hopefully now it is better. If you need a great editor for your book go to http://www.sallyberneathy.com and check her out.

Thank you for purchasing this book, I hope you enjoy it as much as I enjoyed writing them for my faithful readers. Please feel free to email me to tell me what you thought about my stories. I can be reached through http://murdernovels.com thanks again!

The Jim Richards Family of Readers is listed in the back of the book.

Bridezilla Murders
By Bob Moats

Prologue

I hated phone calls in the middle of the night. They either woke me rudely or were bad news. The call at 4 A.M. was bad news.

I rolled over and grabbed the phone, trying to get it before it woke Penny, although she could sleep through a nuclear attack. I almost rolled over Willy, our toy Yorkie, sleeping soundly next to me. He yelped and ran to the foot of the bed. I got to the phone just before its third ring and said hello. It was my brother. I just knew what he was going to tell me. Our father had passed away.

Before I moved in with Penny, I had lived with my parents, helping my mother with my dad who was a stroke victim. His health went downhill over the years after that first stroke, and he didn't get any better after I moved out. I knew it was going to happen one day, but that didn't make it any easier. I hated to see him just sitting in his room watching crappy TV, which was all he seemed to want to do. I

6

would stop by a couple times a week and he was not well, I could tell.

Penny was lying next to me listening to the fragments of my conversation with my brother, and after I hung up and lay back, she pulled me to her. I lay there for what seemed like days.

We were dressed early and on the way to the cemetery two days later, my mom not wanting a funeral, just family and very close friends at the burial. I refused to view my father in the coffin. I wanted to remember him alive, not laid out all made up like a mannequin. Dad was put in the crypt with military honors including a 21 gun salute, and they gave the flag to Mom. We all ended up at a local restaurant for breakfast and then parted to go on with our lives.

Driving back from the restaurant I would glance over at Penny when I could. She was so beautiful to me, and I loved her so much. I was feeling a bit mortal right then. I'm 60 years old and I would never know when I would go out of life as well. We got back to the house, and I took Penny to the living room and sat her down on the couch. I paused a bit too long and she asked if I was all right.

"I'm sad, but what I want to say is something I have thought about for a long time." I paused again. She waited. "We've been together for almost a year now, and I love loving you. You amaze me every day with your silly little skits and shows. I'm always wondering what to expect when I get home. I don't want to lose that."

I got down before her on the couch and said, "I'd be honored if you would be my wife, my love and my life."

Penny's eyes went wide and she got a strange look on her face, happy yet stunned. She took my face in her hands and kissed me fully and firmly. She pulled back and said, "What took you so long?" I laughed and she continued, "I have never met a man quite like you, smart, funny and with a passion for life. Yes, I want to be your wife and have you as my love and my life." She kissed me again.

Chapter 1

I stood, pulled her up and told her to grab Willy's carrier. She did. I put Willy in the doggy purse that I had Penny wear and aimed her for the door. She asked where we were going. I said, you'll see. We got in the car, and I drove over to the Macomb Mall and into Zale's Jewelers. She smiled and said she wanted the biggest rock they had. I said it would be a nice rock. The salesgirl went nuts over Willy then showed us different engagement and wedding rings. We took our time to get it just right.

I still had a huge nest egg from the check I got for the finder's fee from Marsha's embezzlement during the mistress murders, so I didn't care how much the rings cost. We picked out a very nice set and luckily they had them in our sizes. I paid the cashier and we went out.

Penny asked me on the way to our house if we should have a nice quiet wedding, just friends and family, or an elopement to Las Vegas. I laughed and thought about it. Vegas would be nice, and we'd be able to see Deacon and Lynn. I looked at her and asked if she wanted to do that. She said the logistics would be difficult, bringing my mother and family all the way out there, not to mention Buck and Trapper if they wanted to go, but she really did like the idea. We got back to the house and sat talking about how we could pull it off. I got on the phone and called Vegas and got Lynn. It was about 9 A.M. in Vegas and Lynn sounded like she just got up.

"No work today for the wicked?" I asked after putting her on our speaker phone. She recognized my voice, shrieked and called Deacon. I heard him grumbling about being woke so early. I said to Lynn to tell him to get the hell out of bed. Lynn told him who it was, and he bellowed that it was about time I called.

Bridezilla Murders

After they both settled down and put me on their speaker phone, I said, "OK, here's the deal. Penny and I have decided to get married, and we want to do it in Vegas." I waited for them to respond. They did with yelling and screaming. Mostly Deacon was screaming.

Lynn said she had connections with some great wedding planners in Vegas and they would make it an affair to remember. That kind of scared me, but I saw Penny's eyes light up.

"We're still in the planning stages, but we'll let you both know when we're going to attempt it. We have to make sure everyone here can get time off to go, and if we can get them to agree to go out there."

We talked a bit more about life, and I told them about my father. They gave their condolences. We said we'd be in touch soon, said our good-byes and hung up.

Penny had this look on her face that worried me. She looked devious. I asked what was on her evil mind. She said she had an idea to get everyone out to Vegas without having to suffer the airports of hell. I was intrigued, but she said I might not like the idea. I asked her to tell me, and I'd let her know if it was a good idea. She told me to wait and went to the phone in the bedroom, out of my hearing range. I was getting worried.

She was gone for about a half hour while Willy and I sat on the couch waiting. She came bouncing back into the room and said she made a deal with her producer, oh, and he said congratulations, that if the station could film the wedding for the show, they would send everyone out on the corporate jet we flew out in the last time we were in Vegas. I sat looking at her thinking about the circus that this could become, but liked the idea of flying everyone out together for free, and avoiding, as Penny said, the airports of hell. The next thing we would have to attempt was to get everyone to agree on when they were available to go.

I knew my mother had all the time in the world now, but getting her to leave her home and board a plane might be a bit hard to do. My brother was self-employed so he could adjust his life, I hoped. I wanted my son there, but he lived up north, about 250 miles away. I'd see if he could bring his wife and baby down to go with us. This could be a nightmare.

I called Buck and told him our plans, and he whooped and hollered and asked when we were leaving. I said, as soon as I get everyone to settle on dates and times. He said the second check I gave him for guarding Mrs. Truedell and her dog allowed him to have a lot of free time. I said I'd keep him informed.

I called Trapper. I wanted him to come with us. He was good people and he might get a kick out of going back to his home town of Las Vegas.

Bridezilla Murders

"Why do you want to spoil a good thing by getting married, Richards?" Trapper said over the phone when I told him the plan.

"I've wanted to marry Penny for a long time. The events of the last week made me realize life can be short."

"Hey, I'm sorry to hear about your dad. I'll have to see how much vacation time I have. Of course the check you gave me allows for any unpaid time off I'd want, but I may be able to swing it as soon as you let me know when we can go. I think I'd like to go back to my roots, especially go harass my old buddy, Captain Weber." I could see him smiling wide through the phone. We finished, and he hung up.

I looked at Penny and said that today was not a good day to talk to my mom, so soon after the burial, so we'd wait a couple of days and hit her with it. I called my brother and told him. He congratulated us and said it sounded good if the trip was free. I said it would be if we could get everyone together. He said to let him know.

I was feeling like this was not going to be easy. I called my son up in northern Michigan and told him. He said he and his family would love to come. He was unemployed, but I sent a check from my windfall to help them out, and they were free to go. I said they would have to drive down when we decided to go.

Bob Moats

Penny and I sat and drew out a plan on paper then finally came up with an approximate date to make it all happen. It mostly depended on my mom. Penny called her producer, and he said he'd arrange for the jet and the film crew when we had a definite date. The film crew idea still scared me.

We sat back on the couch and soaked in the moment. Penny was admiring her big rock, commenting on how we'd be Mr. and Mrs. soon. She would have to keep her last name due to her show, but she would hyphenate it off the show. Willy was having fits that we were ignoring him. Penny picked him up and rubbed his belly. He forgave us.

~~*~~

The next morning we were up early and dressed. Earlier in the week, Penny had told her producer about the funeral and that she was taking a couple days off. The station would run repeats till she was able to return. We had breakfast. I usually don't, but I was hungry this morning. I guess it had to do with all the pre-marital celebrating we did in bed last night.

I called my mom and said we'd like to stop by. She said she'd like that. We packed up Willy and headed off to see if we could get Mom to leave her home, get on an airplane that she'd never been on before and fly two thousand miles to watch us tie the knot. Mission Impossible.

Bridezilla Murders

We got there and she showered Willy and Penny with hugs and kisses and told us to come and sit. We did and Mom told us how she started cleaning the house and packing away Dad's stuff. She pulled out a small box and gave me a choice of my dad's rings. I picked a nice silver one. My brother would get the gold one.

She said we looked like we had something on our minds. We hesitated, not knowing how she'd take it so soon after the funeral.

"Mom, I realized yesterday that life is precious and I want to make Penny an honest woman, so I asked her to marry me and she accepted." I waited.

Mom went crazy happy and jumped up to hug and kiss Penny, then me. I hated getting sloppy with that kind of happy, but it made Mom feel good. She asked when, and I hesitated again.

"Well, that depends on you. We decided to get married in Las Vegas, and Penny arranged for her station to fly all of us out in the corporate jet to Vegas for free, avoiding commercial airline headaches. I talked to my brother and my son, and they are all for it. We just need to know if you are agreeable to going with us." I paused, waiting for the reasons for her not going so far away.

She surprised me by asking when was the flight out. I told her we still had to arrange it but it would be soon, in a week or so. She said she wouldn't miss it. I looked at Penny and said we had a go for everyone. Now to herd them all into the plane.

Chapter 2

Back at the house I spent some time on the phone getting commitments from everyone to narrow it down to a single date when we would all be available to go. I finally got a date and told Penny. It was to be a week and a half from today. She said that would give her show time to run promos for our big wedding day to be shown on her program. I still had chills about that.

I called Lynn and Deacon and told them when we would be coming out. Penny and I talked about it and decided we would probably be out there at least a week, sending our family back just after the wedding to continue with their lives.

Lynn said she already contacted a wedding planner she knew and gave Penny the number so she could make arrangements. Lynn said they were online with a website and most of the decisions could be made there. Penny said that worked for her. Deacon was yelling in the background that I was an idiot for getting married and should run away fast. Lynn told him to shut up. We talked a little more then hung up.

Penny called the wedding planner and they talked for a good long time. Penny got on the computer, and the wedding planner gave her a tour of the website, guiding her from the phone.

I sat on a chair next to Penny and looked at the tons of wedding crap they offered. I was being amazed by the selection of wedding dresses they had when someone knocked on the front door. I went to answer. It was Trapper.

"Well, what brings out our finest of police detectives today?"

"Yeah, sure, I don't know about the finest. I just stopped by to ask you for a favor." He looked like he wasn't sure if he should ask.

I said, ask away.

"Well, I mentioned to Becker about the wedding, and the boy looked crushed that he hadn't been invited. Is there any way we could fit him in?"

"Crap, I didn't even think about Barry. Wow, let me call him. I'll make it out like I had him on the list, just hadn't got to him yet. I think that will work."

Trapper did something he doesn't do often. He smiled. "I'd like to show him around Vegas, give me something to do while you guys are getting ready for the big event. I know Buck won't want to hang with me. He'll be around you most the time, and I'd feel better with someone along too."

"Will, it's no problem. I like Barry. He's grown on me since the dog watching case. I like the kid. Can he get time off for the trip?"

"I checked on his vacation time, and the idiot hasn't taken off in two years. He has more than enough time to go. Besides, the check you gave him will fill any extra time he needs."

"Good, I'll put him on the guest list and call him shortly."

"Thanks, Jim. I'll leave you two to your...whatever you two do." He smiled again, looked down at Willy and asked if this was his namesake. I realized Trapper hadn't seen the dog yet and lifted Willy up so Trapper could get a closer look. He ruffled Willy's head and said, "You couldn't have named a pitbull after me?" He gave Willy another ruffle and left.

Bridezilla Murders

I put Willy down and went back to Penny who was still on the phone with the wedding planner and still exploring the website. I went out to the kitchen, followed by Willy, and made us something to eat.

After Penny finished, I told her about Trapper's visit. Penny said taking Becker along would be great, she liked him, too. I got on the phone, called him, and said I was just now getting around to calling the people we wanted on our trip. He said he was honored that we thought about him. I told him when the plane flight was planned and he'd need the time off from work. He said he'd arrange it and be there.

Penny and I sat back and talked about what we were getting into. I joked about our wedding becoming a reality show for her program, and I hated reality shows. She smiled and said it was our reality, and that was important to her.

"OK, tell me what you and the long distance wedding planner conspired."

"Well, we're going to the Little Wedding Chapel of Las Vegas to have the wedding. The woman I talked to, her name was Shelby Francis, said that she would call Lynn and arrange for a place to have the reception. There won't be a lot of people there, so we don't need a big place."

I thought about it and figured I might invite a few of my Vegas friends like Wally and the stage crew from the Flamingo Hotel and Casino. Penny said that would be fine with her. I got on the phone again and called Wally. He was happy that we thought about him and the guys and took the information as to when this would all take place. I said I'd call with the final arrangements and would be glad to see them all again. I wondered how Jamie was doing. She was the sister of Lisa who was murdered by Fritz/Wallace during the showgirl murders, and I helped get her a job working stage crew at the Flamingo. I asked, and Wally said Jamie was still working crew and was a joy to work with. I said to be sure to invite her along with the rest of the motley crew. He said he would and we finished.

I thought about inviting Captain Weber from Las Vegas Metro PD. That would make Trapper happy. Penny laughed at the thought of the two of them together and said this was going to be an interesting event. I laughed out loud, and Penny just stared at me. I said we could invite Weber to be an escort for my mom. That would be funny. Penny said Weber was too flighty a person to subject my mom to. I agreed, but it was an idea.

"We'll also need a couple of limos to take everyone to and from the chapel and reception. The film crew will have to arrange for their own transportation." I grinned.

"OK, you're not crazy about the whole taping of our wedding for my show, I understand, but this is going to make things a whole lot easier getting out there. Remember our trip to the Cayman Islands last month. Did you enjoy that plane flight?"

"OK, I yield to your logic. This will make it easier. I'll grin and bear it."

One week later we were zipping around making last minute arrangements for our family to fly out. I hired a stretch limo to take us all to the Detroit City Airport where the corporate jet was stowed. My son said they would drive down that morning and meet us at Penny's house. Penny was flitting around getting packed, and I warned her to cut back on the suitcases. She managed to only pack three this time. She did manage to pack only one suitcase for Willy, but I think she slipped some of her things in that bag, too.

"OK, we get to Vegas on Wednesday, then we'll have three days to get ready for the wedding on Saturday afternoon. Lynn and Deacon said they have a banquet room at the MGM Grand reserved and they will be set up by the time we roll in after the wedding. I reserved suites for everyone in the MGM Grand, which cost a small fortune. I can afford it, but it was still a bit of a bite. Having the reception there would also make it easier for everyone to get to their rooms. I doubled up Becker and Trapper in one room, my brother and his wife in another, and my son and family in another. Oh, and I put my mother in with my brother. That should make him happy. We're the ones getting married so why are we doing all the work?"

Penny looked at me and asked, "Did you get us a room?"

I grinned and said, "Yes, the honeymoon suite at the Bellagio Hotel. I don't want to be anywhere near my family on my wedding night."

Penny laughed and asked where Buck was staying. I said Deacon had told his sister Maria about her invitation to the wedding, and she asked if Buck was coming. He said yes, of course, so Maria wanted Buck to stay at her place. I talked to Buck, and he said that was fine with him. I knew it would be.

The next day Penny came back from her station bearing gifts. She said her station threw a bridal shower for her and they put it on her show. I helped her bring in the gifts and then we went to see the TiVo of the show. I still felt weird about having our wedding broadcast on TV but it was a tradeoff. Her show made a big deal about the wedding, and Penny said she'd be gone for a week in Vegas then back to show everyone her wedding video.

Wednesday morning came quickly. My son, his wife and my grandson arrived around 7 A.M. Shortly after, my brother came rolling in with his wife. He also picked up our mother. Mom was really hopped up over going on this trip and said so. Penny was going all nuts over my grandson, Alex, holding him as if he was hers. I didn't think she'd give him back. Trapper and Becker came in by 7:30 A.M. followed shortly by Buck. I had hired a stretch limo. It came by 8 A.M., and we all piled in with Willy in a metal dog carrier. The limo company also sent a van to follow us with the luggage that wouldn't fit in the limo. We headed down I-94 to Detroit City Airport and found the jet all ready to go. I was surprised to see the same pilots and flight attendant from our last trip to Vegas. I guess they were company people.

The film crew was already there. They amounted to one camera man, a sound man, one equipment handler and a woman who would be the director of this little project. She knew Penny so they greeted each other as the cameraman was taking his videos of our arrival at the terminal. I was still not crazy about having my life on a reality show. Oh well.

Chapter 3

Penny was still carrying my grandson, soon to be our grandson, and was directing everyone to the jet. I carried Willy's prison onto the plane, and everyone was aboard and seated as the flight attendant gave us the standard flight briefing. We all buckled in for the takeoff. Willy's carrier was strapped to the back floor where they usually put wheelchairs. The camera crew was busy recording everything for posterity.

The jet taxied out to the runway and was given clearance to go. I loved to fly, not commercial, but this private jet was great. We were airborne and my mother was excited watching out the window as the ground dropped below us. At 80 years old, she had never gone up in a plane, let alone a jet. She was glued to the window watching the scenery fly by below.

Penny retrieved her future grandson from my daughter-in-law and was talking to him, poor kid. We all gabbed and enjoyed the trip. We let Willy loose, and he cuddled up to everyone. Then about half way across the states I gave everyone a rundown of how this attack on Vegas would go. I explained the room set-ups and where we would be for the wedding and reception.

Trapper joked about having to be in the same room with Becker. I said he could pay for his own room if he didn't like the arrangements. He said that he'd put up with Becker, but only if he behaved. Becker would have given Trapper the finger, but there were women and children aboard.

About three and a half hours later the co-pilot came out and told us we would be landing shortly so we should all take our seats. We landed in Las Vegas at

Bridezilla Murders

McCarran International Airport without a bump and were all herded off the jet into a waiting stretch limo for our journey to the MGM Grand. The camera crew had a van waiting for them and followed us. We arrived and I told the driver to leave Penny's and my baggage and the doggy carrier in the car and wait for us. The driver agreed and parked off to the side. Penny had Willy in his doggy purse for the trip into the hotel.

The camera crew was still recording, but not too close, thankfully, all the way into the hotel lobby. People around us were wondering what was going on since we departed a limo and had a camera crew recording our every move. I kind of felt like a celebrity. One woman asked me if we were famous. I pointed to Willy and said that he was Lassie. She bought it and went to tell her husband.

I took everyone to the registration desk and got them all assigned to their suites then we went up to them. They were all next to each other, and I had asked the hotel for the best rooms with a good view of the strip. I was happy with their choice. My mom was like a little kid at her first circus, just about bouncing up and down. I looked at my brother and said to have fun. He just smiled and rolled his eyes.

After everyone was shown to their rooms, I gathered everybody in Trapper's room and told them that Trapper was to be in charge if there were problems. I told them Penny and I would be back shortly after we checked into our hotel. I wasn't telling anyone where we were staying; that was to be a closely guarded secret. I made sure everyone had their cell phones with them and turned on in case I had to call.

I took Buck and Penny back down to the limo and had the driver take Buck to Maria's where we said our hellos. Maria jumped all over Penny, congratulating her and me. I told Maria where to bring the two of them for dinner tonight. I said I'd call with more details and then had the driver take Penny and me to the Bellagio Hotel where we got registered. We went up to the suite, and I was impressed with the view, right over the fountain. Willy was right at home, jumped up on the couch and curled up to sleep. I called Trapper to make sure everyone was behaving, and he said all was well. I told him we'd be back there to go to dinner around 5:00 and to have everyone ready.

I called Lynn and Deacon. They were excited that we were in and settled. I told them where we would be having dinner for our first night in town, and they said they'd be there.

Penny and I had about an hour and a half before going back to the MGM Grand, so we made good use of the time on the huge bed. I noticed there was no whirlpool spa by the window like we had last time we were in Vegas at the MGM; here it was back in the bathroom. It didn't matter. We would be busy entertaining our family.

Around 4:30 we called for a room sitter for Willy. They sent one up, and we gathered ourselves, went back to the MGM Grand, and herded our group to go to dinner. We went down to the area of the hotel set up for any kind of restaurant you'd want. The restaurant I chose had our table ready for our group, and the hostess asked the camera crew not to film while in the restaurant. I wanted to cheer the hostess. The cameraman did manage to sneak over with one of those tiny digital video cameras and recorded as much as he could before the hostess caught on and chased him out again. She was on my Christmas list.

Deacon and Lynn arrived, and I introduced them to my family. Trapper latched on to Deacon with a bear hug that surprised me and, I think, Deacon too. Deacon introduced Lynn to Trapper and Becker and then they took their seats. Everyone ordered and while waiting for the food to come we sat and talked.

Trapper stood and clinked his glass with a fork, getting everyone's attention.

"I was there when Jim and Penny reunited for the first time in forty years, at the TV station after she received the death threat. Deacon was there, too. That was the start of our adventure that led us to this week. I want to say that even though I'm not best man—" he gave a fake cough— "I want to be the first to officially congratulate them on their wedding."

Everyone applauded and Trapper sat down. I was impressed by his short speech, and then Buck stood. "I've known Jim for a couple of years and Penny almost a year and I am honored to be the best man." He grinned at Trapper. "I hope Penny and Jim have a long and happy life together now that they are not going to be living in sin anymore." He grinned as everyone laughed. He held up his glass and proposed a toast. Everyone joined, and then our food arrived.

We ate and afterwards we all headed up to Trapper's room, called for room service, plenty of beer and pop, and partied till about 2 A.M. when we started losing people to sleep. Mom was the first to go, followed by my son and his family. My brother and wife hung in, but finally they left, too. Buck and Maria left around 3 A.M. then Deacon and Lynn left to get rested for tomorrow. They had each taken time off from their police duties to be with us. Penny and Lynn had plotted to go get Penny fitted for the dress tomorrow at the bridal boutique owned by Shelby Francis, the wedding planner.

Trapper, Becker, Penny and I sat for a short time, then Penny and I left to go back to our suite at the Bellagio. Outside the room I told Trapper where we were staying but swore him to an oath he wouldn't tell anyone unless there was an emergency.

Bridezilla Murders

We got back to our room and just crashed on the bed. We were too tired to fool around so we just slept. Willy was sound asleep at the end of the bed before I even drifted off.

Next morning around 7:30 Lynn was banging on our door. I was surprised to see her.

"How did you find us?" I asked.

She grinned and said, "I'm a good detective." I laughed over her use of my favorite line. "And I have a badge," she added and laughed.

Penny and Lynn cackled like hens, and I asked where Deacon was. Lynn said he'd be along shortly to keep me busy while the girls did their thing. They went out, and Willy and I stood by the window looking out at the strip, wishing we lived here. I called Trapper and asked how everyone was doing. He said they all gathered and went down for breakfast. He said my mom was a ball of energy, all over the place in the mall area of the hotel. I laughed and asked him to keep an eye on her; he said he would.

There was a knock on the door; it was Deacon. "Well, are you ready to go escort my family around Vegas?"I asked. He smiled and said he alerted the police that there was a crazy bunch of terrorist tourists in town. I put Willy in his doggy purse, and

Deacon made fun of me for wearing such a cute purse. I stuck my tongue out at him and we went out.

I had asked Deacon to rent a large van with windows all around to haul my family around Vegas. He rented a monster of a stretch van that he parked at the valet parking, showing them his badge and warning the valet attendants that if anyone touched the van it would be fatal for them. We went to the MGM Grand where my friends and family agreed to meet us at the valet parking in front. Trapper knew the area well and had everyone waiting there when we pulled up.

Chapter 4

I took Deacon aside and told him I was going to take Trapper and Becker over to Metro Police and see if we could stir up Captain Weber. Deacon said that neither he nor Lynn had said a word about Trapper coming into town, so it would be a surprise. I asked Deacon if he could take everyone to catch the afternoon show of Ron Lucas, the ventriloquist, and we'd catch up to them later. I gave him enough cash to buy everyone tickets and went to tell my family what was happening. They all loved the idea of seeing the show, so Deacon piled everyone into the van.

Buck said he and Maria wanted to go wander the strip, and I said that worked for me. Then I asked them if they would watch Willy for me. Maria was all excited to take the dog. She slung the doggy purse over her head and they walked off heading over to Las Vegas Boulevard. I could see Willy's head looking back at me, probably thinking, what the hell is going on?

I went into the MGM Grand followed by Trapper and Becker, over to the car rental booth and got an SUV like the one I had last time we were here. They brought the car around and we climbed in. I drove over to Tropicana Boulevard and up to Metro Police. Trapper was like a little kid seeing his hometown again.

"Damn building hasn't changed at all since I left," he said as we pulled into the parking lot of Metro PD. I parked and we all headed to the front door just as two officers were coming out. They froze and one of them yelled, "Crap, we got trouble, call SWAT."

Everyone laughed, and the officer who yelled ran to Trapper and gave him a bear hug. Trapper started to wrestle with the cop and then they broke loose.

"What the hell you doing in town? I thought Weber told you never to set foot back here." The cop speaking was introduced to me and Becker as Sergeant Tim Carney, a good friend from Trapper's past.

"You know I don't play by the rules." Trapper laughed.

"Weber's going to crap when he sees you. Does he know you're in town?"

"Nope, this is going to be a total surprise."

"Come on in, Will. I'll get on the horn and call Weber out. I want to see the look on his face." Carney put his arm around Trapper and took him in. The lobby went a bit nuts from the officers who had known Trapper, and it was like a party. Carney got on the phone and called Weber, telling him there was someone here to see him. Trapper stepped behind me as Weber came out. He saw me and got a big grin.

"Richards, you're back in town. Pleasure or business?" he bellowed.

Behind me Trapper said, "We're here for pleasure," then popped his head around me and smiled at Weber.

Weber just stared and quietly said, "Oh, shit." I could see the veins on his head growing, and he bellowed even louder, "What the hell you doing in my town? I had hoped I'd never see you again."

Trapper came around me, went nose to nose with Weber and said, "Did you think you could keep me out of my home town, you old-should-have-retired-years-ago dinosaur!"

Weber just stared Trapper down, then laughed heartily and gave Trapper a hug, almost lifting him off the ground.

"You crooked son of a bitch, how are you doing?" Weber was relaxed now.

"I'm doing great. You already know Richards. This other idiot is one of my boys from back in Michigan, Officer Barry Becker. He came out here to help me stir up trouble." Trapper was enjoying this.

Weber came to Becker, shook his hand and said, "I feel so sorry for you. I'll tell you some stories about this man that will curl your hair." He loved those stories. I tend to believe they were the best times he had in his cop career.

"Captain Weber, I'm in town to marry Penny Wickens. You remember her?" I asked.

"I sure do remember that pretty little lady. About time you latched hold of her."

"Well, I'd like to invite you to the wedding or, if it's easier for you, the reception."

He was almost speechless. "I'm honored to be invited. Thank you so much for thinking of me. Do you want a police honor guard for your wedding? I can have them bring their swords."

"No, thank you. It's going to be a simple ceremony, just my family and friends. If you want to bring a date or your wife if you're married, that would be fine."

"No wife and no woman would want me for a date. Had enough of women, not wanting to get into that again." He gave out that deep throaty laugh of his, and I figured my mom would be safe from him.

"Well, you are invited with or without a date." I smiled. He congratulated me and then said he had work to do.

He said out loud in the lobby to all the officers nearby, "I want every man here to get a good look at this man." He pointed to Trapper. "If you see him so much as jaywalk, I want him hauled in and booked." He smiled, punched Trapper's arm and said to come back again for a talk.

Trapper said he would, and Weber went back into his office after saying good bye to Becker and me. Trapper stood around talking to his old friends and telling them about his adventures in boring Michigan. Most of the cops there had heard about the classmate murders incident, so Trapper had to talk about that for a bit. I just snickered at how Trapper was saying he saved the day with his quick thinking and cop work.

My cell phone rang. It was Deacon saying the show ended and they were all going to Sonic Burgers for lunch. I asked which one and said we'd meet them there. I pulled Trapper away from his admiring audience, and we departed the place.

Trapper was in heaven now. We got to the Sonic Burger and found Deacon's van. Luckily there was an open space next to him. We pulled in and ordered through the speaker. My family all told me how good the show was. My mom especially liked it. The food came out with the roller skating girls, and we ate what I considered the best burgers around.

~~*~~

Lynn and Penny were in the fitting room trying on the gown Penny had picked out from the website. Penny was speechless over the dress, and Lynn was kidding about pinning down Deacon for a wedding just so she could wear one of these beautiful gowns. The camera crew was allowed to tape Penny after she was dressed. They were taping just as Shelby Francis, the bridal boutique owner, came in and greeted Lynn who introduced Penny. Shelby had watched Penny's show and was honored that her boutique would be featured on the show. Shelby told Penny that she would donate the gown if her store would get a mention in the credits on her show. Penny looked overwhelmed and said that was doable then asked Lonie, the video director, if they could get a shot of the front of the building. She agreed and told the crew to get the shot before they left. Shelby was ecstatic and told her employees to give Penny the royal treatment.

They were still getting the dress sized when a woman burst into the fitting room screaming about how she was supposed to be getting fitted for her gown. The employee told her it would be a few minutes more, then she would be taken care of. The woman screamed that she wasn't to be treated like a second rate customer, started swearing and demanded to see the owner. Lynn was just about ready to pull her badge, tell the woman to cool her jets or be hauled in for disturbing the peace, when Shelby came flying back in.

The woman hadn't noticed the camera crew was taping her tirade, and Shelby tried to calm her by telling her that she could use the main fitting room. The woman then started bitching about the material of the gown she selected, saying it was too scratchy, she wanted better, and if she didn't get better treatment, she would go elsewhere. Shelby had another employee take the woman to an empty room to start her fitting. Shelby apologized to Penny and said that she was an example of the Bridezilla, and so far this one was the queen of them all. She had Bridezillas in numerous times and, as much as she hated them, they paid.

Penny told Shelby that in the past she had wedding planners on her show and they had told tales of the Bridezilla, so she understood. Shelby said that this one actually dragged her future husband in and put him down so much while they were deciding on the food menu that he was almost in tears. She treated her bridesmaids worse, and her future mother-in-law stormed out earlier telling Shelby that she hated her son's bitch. Shelby just gave a little chuckle.

They could still hear the woman screaming in the next room, something about the bridesmaids' gowns being hideous, and she wanted to see the owner. The female employee came back almost in tears and asked if Shelby could come back to the main fitting room. Shelby went out. Lonie, the video director, was whispering to the cameraman that this was video gold.

Penny said to Lynn that she felt sorry for Shelby. They could still hear the Bridezilla screaming for everyone to get out while she changed clothes. The room went quiet for about two minutes before Lynn and Penny were surprised by what sounded like a gunshot.

Chapter 5

Lynn pulled her gun out from under her jacket and ran out of the fitting room, followed by Penny still in her dress. The camera crew came up fast. A crowd had gathered by the door to the other fitting room, and Lynn, holding up her badge, called out for everyone to get back. They dispersed, and she went in. The Bridezilla was lying in a pool of blood that was being soaked up by her wedding dress. Lynn checked her vitals and said she was dead. Shelby came running in and was shocked by the sight. Lynn went out to a phone and called it in. The camera crew was taping everything; it now looked like an episode of "Cops." Lonie was thinking two episodes on Penny's show, one of the wedding and one of the crime. She loved it and got on her cell phone to call the producer. Lynn came back and told them to get out of the crime scene before she had them all arrested.

~~*~~

We had just finished our lunch and were getting ready to drive up to Fremont Street when my cell phone rang. It was Penny. I answered. She was calmly telling me what happened when Deacon's cell phone rang. I presumed it was Lynn. Deacon looked at me as I was talking to Penny and nodded. We finished our calls, and I took Trapper aside and asked him and Becker if they would escort my family around Fremont Street. I filled them in on the sketchy details. Trapper said he'd be happy to. I apologized to the family and told them Penny needed me to go over wedding details at the bridal boutique. I didn't want to alarm them with the gory details. Deacon and I got into the SUV and drove over to the bridal boutique. We arrived, and I saw Detective Williams outside. I knew him from the showgirl murders.

He saw me and smiled. "We got a murder. I just knew you were back in town." He laughed and shook my hand. I asked how Nicky North was doing. He said they got him a sentence of ten years. Nicky was one of the principle troublemakers in the showgirl murders here in Vegas and part of a drug-running ring. Penny almost killed him with my gun when he tried to shoot me. Ah, the good memories.

Deacon and I went in and found Lynn and Penny, who had changed out of her dress so I wouldn't see it. Deacon was now part of homicide so he and Lynn went into the crime scene.

Penny put her arms around me. "The victim was causing all kinds of trouble for everyone. She was a Bridezilla." I knew the term. "They took her into the room and she was screaming at everyone then chased everyone out of her room, and that's when we heard the shot. Lynn got to the room, but the bride was the only one in there, alone."

I went to the door of the fitting room and looked in as CSI was taking pictures and making their examinations. The bride was still on the floor, and Lynn and Deacon were talking at the back of the room as the ME was checking the body. I turned to see the camera crew was documenting everything. Ah, reality shows.

I went back to Penny. Shelby came up and Penny introduced me. I said this was not a good start for our wedding, I was just glad it wasn't Penny.

"I don't think Penny was in any danger. This woman was a royal bitch and was not loved by a good number of people. I'm surprised she made it this far. Pardon me, I don't mean to speak ill of the dead. It's just too bad it had to happen here." She excused herself when Lynn and Deacon came out of the room and went to talk to Lynn.

"I haven't had a lot of time with you or my family. I hope this doesn't get in the way," I said.

Lynn came over and said they had the fiancé and the bridesmaids in a separate room. She asked me if I wanted to give my take on her questioning. I said I would. She wanted to do some interrogation here while it was still fresh. We went to the room. Lynn stopped the camera crew and said it was off limits to them, then she asked if the groom would come into a separate office. He had already been checked for gunshot residue and was clean. Deacon sat next to Lynn as I stood at the back of the office ready for the grilling. I missed the two-way mirror.

Lynn introduced herself, then Deacon, and said I was a civilian advisor.

"Your name is?"

"Michael Rawlings. Annamarie was my fiancé." He sat straight and looked calm, strange for a man whose fiancé was just brutally murdered.

"Is there any reason that someone would want to murder your fiancé?"

He looked like he wasn't sure how to answer that question. "I'm sorry. I loved Annamarie, but she could be a bit mean to people. I don't know who was angry enough at her to do this, but I'm sure she pissed off a few people."

I thought that he was being open about the woman, but he still seemed a bit too cool about it all. He definitely didn't seem like a grieving bridegroom.

"Where were you when Annamarie was shot?" Lynn asked.

"I was in the waiting room. She told me that I wasn't allowed in to watch the fitting. You know, bad luck seeing the dress before the wedding. She insisted I come in today to settle the other details of the wedding and reception," he said calmly.

Lynn asked him a few more routine questions and cut him loose with a warning that he would be called in again for further questioning. He went out, and I said I almost thought he was relieved that she was dead, but I didn't think he had it in him to commit the deed. Lynn and Deacon agreed.

Lynn questioned the four girls who made up the bridesmaids, and all had the same reaction, like they weren't upset by her death. I told Lynn that maybe they all conspired to murder her. Lynn laughed and said she only heard one gun shot. I asked if she was going to question the employees. Penny said they were a bit put off by Bridezillas. Lynn said she would but later.

The lead CSI came in and said they were done and the ME had carted out the body. Lynn went out and told Shelby that the room would have to be shut off from people using it for now. She asked Shelby if she saw the mother-in-law actually leave the building, and was there any way she could have slipped back in without being seen. Shelby said that her girls would have noticed her. There were only a few entrances to the building that couldn't be seen by her employees. Lynn thanked Shelby and came back to us. Penny was holding on to my arm tightly. Lynn said there was not much else to do till they got something from forensics. The room had no windows, only one entrance, and no one saw anyone come out of the room after the gun shot. This would be a puzzle.

Lynn turned and stopped, yelling, "If you don't get that camera out of my face I'll take you in for something!" The cameraman put his camera down and smiled, then Lonie said they had enough.

Shelby asked Penny and me if we wanted to discuss the wedding plans, and I figured since we were both there, why not. Lynn and Deacon said they were going back to the station to file their reports and would catch up to us later.

Penny and I picked out the cake and went over the menu for food, table dressings and flowers. I had to call Wally to find out how many people he had on the list I had asked him to get for guests from the stage crew so we could have a definite head count. He gave me the info and I said we'd see him Saturday. Penny and I finished up on the details, and Shelby said her people would have it all for us by Saturday at the banquet hall in the MGM Grand.

We stood and thanked Shelby for all she was doing for us, then we turned to go out the door of the office, followed by the camera crew still taping. In the hallway we all stopped when a woman rushed by us screaming about her fiancé having a bachelor party that had a stripper. She was swearing that she would make his life miserable. She was yelling for service, she had a wedding to plan and it better be right or someone would pay. She went into an office still screaming about the crappy service she was getting here. Shelby looked at us with a sad face, apologized, then went to calm the woman.

I looked at Penny and said that we should get out of there before that Bridezilla got murdered, too. We left and headed back to the MGM Grand. The crew van followed. I called Trapper, and he said everyone was gathered in his room and was having a nice time talking about their day. He did say to rescue him so he and Becker could go do some fun things around Vegas. I said we'd be there shortly to take over and hung up.

I looked at Penny and said Trapper was going to go out and get in trouble, I could feel it.

Chapter 6

We went up to Trapper's room. I greeted everyone and said that Penny and I had everything ready for Saturday. Penny, of course, latched onto our grandson. Buck and Maria were back, so Willy jumped on my leg wanting attention. I lifted him and gave him a good nuzzle. He wiggled happily and tried to lick my face. I said, "No doggy kisses, don't kiss, doggy," imitating Soupy Sales from my childhood.

Trapper pulled me aside and asked what happened at the bridal salon. I told him Penny and I got all the wedding details finished up. He looked at me, snarled and said that I knew what he meant. I laughed and gave him the gory details of the murder. He was thinking about the fact that the room was vacant of anyone else except the dead body. He asked me if there was any kind of opening or window. I said no, there weren't any openings someone could have fired a gun through. He smiled and said it was Deacon and Lynn's problem, and he wanted to take Becker out for a little fun on the town. I said to have fun, but please be back for the wedding and call if I needed to bail him out. He laughed and said they wouldn't catch him. That had me worried.

Trapper picked up a small bag, asked to me to lock up his suite, grabbed Becker and they went out of the room then disappeared down the hallway. Penny came up to me. We looked like the typical family— man, woman, child and dog. I asked if anyone had a camera and had my son start taking pictures with my Fuji camera.

Maria was sitting on Buck's lap on the couch, and my mother was standing looking out the window over the strip. I came to her and asked what she thought about it all. She said she wasn't fond of the heat, but it was beautiful. I asked if everyone was interested in seeing the world's largest gift shop to get some souvenirs. They all responded positively. We went down to the van and drove over to the gift store on Sahara and the Boulevard. The camera crew followed. We explored the place for about an hour. After everyone bought up their remembrance articles, I gathered everyone and headed back to the hotel to relax and get ready for dinner. Maria and Buck left to go to her home to change, saying they would be back later.

My brother told me that he and his wife had been in Vegas once before and thanked me for bringing them out again. I sat with my son and his wife and talked a bit about what was going on in their lives. My mom went into her bedroom to take a short nap before the evening events.

Penny was still playing with little Alex, and I told her that we should go to our suite and get ready. She probably would have brought the baby with us, but I said that she should leave him to his mother. She surrendered him reluctantly, and I said we'd be back around 5 to go to dinner. I didn't mention that I had reservations to see the Blue Man Group. I wanted it to be a surprise.

We got back to the Bellagio and relaxed a bit, then there was a knock at the door. It was Deacon and Lynn. They came in and we all sat talking.

"Forensics is doing their magic on the evidence but won't have anything soon. I'm baffled how someone could be shot in an enclosed room without the killer being seen. Unless everyone was too preoccupied to see anything or just happy she was taken out. No one saw a thing." Lynn didn't sound happy.

"Well, a murder is not in our schedule of happy events for the next two days until Penny and I take the oath of love. Murder is not part of that oath, I hope." I smiled as Penny agreed.

"Has Trapper gone on his rampage yet?" Deacon asked.

"He left with Becker about an hour ago. I've been waiting for a call to rescue him from jail." I laughed.

"Trapper loved to pull practical jokes around the Clinton Township precinct, and I feel sorry for the beat cops here for the next couple days," he said with a smile. "One time back in Michigan he managed to rearrange the captain's office, turning everything around facing the back of the room. Captain was not happy, but after he cooled, he appreciated the effort and thought that went into it. Never did nail Trapper for it. Trapper's crafty, never got caught in the past."

"Yeah, I heard it took Weber about two months before he found out someone was running a call girl ring right in the jail." Lynn laughed. "But he never could prove it was Trapper."

"I wonder how he stayed a cop all these years." I was amazed.

"Like I said, he never got caught." Deacon smiled.

My cell phone rang, and it was Trapper. He excused himself and Becker from dinner and said they'd see us later. I said it was no problem and hung up. I told everyone what Trapper said. Deacon exclaimed that the fun was beginning.

We called for a sitter for Willy, and after she arrived we went and met the family at the MGM hotel. Everyone piled into the van with me driving, the camera crew trying to keep up in their van. We went to the Hofbrauhaus restaurant, had a good German meal, and sang along with the German band. The restaurant manager asked the camera crew not to disturb his customers, so the cameraman used his tiny digital camera again. That was accepted by the manager. After the meal I announced that we were going to see the Blue Man Group and everyone cheered.

We piled into the van, and the camera crew said that they'd call it a night. They wanted to explore Vegas before their work was over and they had to go back to Michigan. I thought that was a great idea and told them to go have fun.

At the theatre we sat and enjoyed the Blue Man Group show. One of the Blue Men startled my mom by walking across the backs of the seat till he got to her then looking down at her. She cringed, and he went on walking over her head to the seats behind us.

After the show I took everyone up to Fremont Street to watch the overhead video that ran down the street for over two blocks. We watched the show then explored the mall, watching the vendors displaying their wares and going into a couple of casinos so my mother could try her luck at the slots. She actually won a couple of dollars and wanted to go again, but I said she should hold on to her winnings. She'd just lose it back to the casino.

Back out on the street there was a jazz band playing on the small stage that they had on one side of the enclosed street. We stood watching them for a while. By this time a new show started overhead, and we watched the new video. Penny held me tightly and whispered in my ear that she remembered the first time I brought her here and we stood watching the show. After it ended, we all went back to the van and drove down the strip looking at all the lights flashing and moving. My mother was thoroughly impressed and said she could see why I loved this town.

The evening ended well. I got everyone back to the hotel where my brother and his wife said they were going to walk uptown and explore the strip some more. They asked my mother to join them, but she decided to go back to the room and relax. My son and wife decided to call it a night also, so they escorted Mom up to her room. Buck and Maria headed off into the night to do whatever they wanted. I felt sorry for Buck.

Deacon and Lynn came with us to the Bellagio to relax and get some room service. I tipped the girl who watched Willy for us. Willy went back to his space on the couch, circled and plopped down, worn out from the day.

Around 10:15 Lynn's cell phone rang and she answered, listened for a few minutes then hung up.

"That was Williams. He said they got a call around 6:00 from a distraught man saying his fiancé hadn't come back to the hotel. She was last seen at Shelby's boutique. He called there and they said she left around 4:00, and they didn't see where she went. The officer who took the call told the man that she may have gone exploring Vegas and to call back if she didn't return later. Around 7:30 one of Shelby's employees went to take out the trash and found the bride in the dumpster with a knife stabbed through the heart. ME and CSI have been on the scene for the last couple hours. Williams thought he'd let me know, that it might be connected to my Bridezilla murder.

Williams talked to Shelby, and she said the woman was another Bridezilla."

Chapter 7

Lynn asked Penny and me if we wanted to tag along on a boring murder investigation. Penny was all excited to be included and packed up Willy to go. We all headed out in my SUV since it had more room for all of us than Lynn's Pontiac Vibe. I was amazed that Deacon would even be seen in such a small car, but Lynn defended it as a good running and a comfortable vehicle. Deacon made no comment.

We arrived at Shelby's bridal boutique and found Williams standing out back grinning from ear to ear.

"Boy, Richards, when you come to town they all drop dead." He made a motion of hanging himself, and Lynn said, why don't you do that?

We found Shelby in her office looking totally distraught. She said she was worried this would kill her business. I thought, not as much as killing her clients, but I kept my mouth shut. Williams told Lynn she could take the lead since it probably was connected to the earlier Bridezilla murder. Lynn sat by Shelby and told her to relax.

"Now tell me everything that happened from the time this woman came to the boutique," Lynn said.

"Well, she arrived just before Jim and Penny were finished with their wedding arrangements. We came out of the office, and this woman, Becky Taylor, came past us screaming that her fiancé had a stripper at his bachelor party and she was going to make his life miserable. Then she made our lives miserable with her demands. She made all the plans for the wedding without her fiancé, got fitted for her gown, complaining all the while, and then she finished around 4 P.M. and we were glad to see her go. That was the last we saw of her until Mindy took the trash out and found her in the dumpster. Oh, god, poor Mindy, she'll never get over this."

"Her fiancé was never here, never included in the wedding planning?" Lynn asked.

"No, he was not here, just the bridesmaids. The woman's mother came in briefly and then left. I don't really think she wanted to have anything to do with her daughter's wedding plans. She called her a real bitch, sorry to speak ill of the dead, but that's what her own mother said."

"You never saw her or the bridesmaids after they left? No one came back?"

"No, I thought we were done with her until the wedding."

"Did Taylor leave by herself or with the bridesmaids?"

"Well, I think the bridesmaids had enough of her, so they left after being fitted for their gowns. Becky Taylor left by herself and did mention that she had a rental car since she was in town for just the wedding."

Lynn looked at Deacon and said to check the parking lot to see if her rental was still there. He went out, and Lynn thanked Shelby then said she was sorry for all that happened today. Shelby looked at Penny and me and said she hoped this wouldn't look bad on Penny's show. Penny said she'd try to down play it all. Shelby thanked her.

We all went outside after Lynn went around to the employees who were still attending to their closing chores and asked them a few questions. I was amazed that the camera crew was there taping the whole dumpster exam. I asked Lonie how they knew that we were there, and she said they were listening to the police scanner, recognized the bridal boutique and stopped by, thinking there was a connection, and there was. Deacon came back in and said there were no unaccounted cars in the lot; the rental car must have been taken. Lynn said to check with all the rental agencies to see who rented it to Taylor and what happened to the car. Deacon told another detective to follow the rental lead and report back. He looked at me and said it was good to be in charge.

We all stood out in the parking lot, Lynn looking frustrated.

"I hate to say it but I think Shelby or one of her employees is involved," I offered.

Lynn looked at me with weary eyes and asked why.

"Well, stands to reason. I'm sure you've already thought of this. Two unrelated cases of murder in the same location, murder of two Bridezillas, who didn't know each other. What's the connection? The only link is the bridal boutique. Just my opinion," I offered again.

"I like Shelby. I've known her since my first and only marriage, and I can't imagine her doing this. Maybe one of the employees, fed up with the bitching, snapped and acted out. They have access to the rooms and the women. Maybe one of them did the deed."

"Well, there are two murders, two murderers or one. Maybe the second killing was inspired by the first, whatever. Two cases to solve," I said.

Williams came up and said, "You're going to love this. ME came back with a preliminary COD. She was stabbed with a cake knife. That's appropriate." He laughed and walked off.

"I hate Williams," Lynn said under her breath.

The CSI finished with the dumpster and the surrounding area and found nothing more. They closed up and went off to do their thing back at the crime lab. The camera crew said they were going back to exploring Vegas. We were wearing down and left the scene after Lynn made sure everyone was finished there. We drove back to the Bellagio. Lynn and Deacon begged off for being too wiped out, went to their car and drove home. Penny, Willy and I went up to our room and crashed into the bed after quickly undressing, ready to sleep.

"Are we getting so old we wear out after such a day? I don't feel like fooling around for the second night in a row. Damn, we're here to get married, and we should be fooling around all over the place," I lamented.

"Oh, shut up and quit complaining. Go to sleep," Penny mimicked like an old married woman.

"Yep, now we sound like we're about to be married," I joked.

Penny swung her leg over me and said, don't count on it. We kicked Willy out of the bedroom. He wasn't happy, but we were.

Friday morning came early. We lay around until the sun burst through the bedroom window of the honeymoon suite. Deacon called around 8 A.M. and said they were ready to go take the family exploring if we were ready. I said we needed breakfast and would be at the MGM around 10. Lynn came on the phone and said to look out my window. She waited while I walked to the window overlooking the fountain. Today the water was pink. I asked if that was natural. She said no, someone dumped in a whole lot of red food coloring and turned the water pink. I thought of Trapper and Becker and laughed. I asked if she was thinking what I was. She said, most likely.

We were up and dressed, and Willy was mad at us that he couldn't sleep in the bed. We took him down for his walk and to take a dump, then we went to get breakfast.

Deacon came by our room around 9:45 and said that Lynn would join us later; she was called in to report to Weber about the murders. Seems there were some important people in town who wanted the case solved quickly. They didn't want the tourists to be afraid to get married in Vegas.

Bridezilla Murders

Penny and I gathered our stuff and packed Willy in his purse. Deacon still joked about my wearing the thing. I smiled at him, took the doggy purse off, and slung it around Deacon who stood still not wanting to do anything to hurt the tiny dog. I said, now Willy should be safe with such a big protector, and turned to go out. Deacon started to protest, but Penny said he looked so handsome with the dog. Deacon smiled and looked down at Willy who was looking up at Deacon. He said, this is not so bad, and we all went out.

We got down to the lobby and I saw two Metro officers talking to a couple of suits. I recognized one officer as Sergeant Carney, Trapper's friend. He saw me and waved. I took my troops over, and Carney smiled at Deacon, saying he liked the dog, that he had a Yorkie, too. Deacon sighed a breath of relief that he wasn't going to be subjected to jokes. I asked Carney what was up, and he said they were called in to investigate the coloring of the fountain; he just smiled. I had a feeling he knew who did it, but that was a subject for investigation. He said the perps moved around the security cameras, like they knew where they were. Then they dumped in a couple of gallons of red food coloring, being diluted by the tremendous amount of water to come out pink. I was trying not to laugh, as I'm sure Carney was as well.

Score one for the Vegas Jokers.

Chapter 8

We arrived at the MGM and went up to my family's floor. I banged on Trapper's door but there was no answer; he was probably hiding out. My brother gathered his wife and our mother and came out to the hallway. My son and family were ready, also. Penny, of course, latched onto the baby.

"Today we are going to take a helicopter ride over Vegas. I made reservations for the flight, so if everyone is ready, we can go after I call Buck and Maria."

Deacon spoke up and said that Maria called him earlier to say she and Buck were going to take a trip up to Mt. Charleston for a picnic. I said that worked, and herded everyone to the elevators.

We went down to where the helicopter rides were located and had to put everyone on two helicopters. Deacon and I held back as there was still not enough room, so I told everyone to enjoy the ride and we'd wait here. Penny, still holding the baby, went with my son and his wife and my mother in the other copter. They lifted off and I could see the expression on my mom's face, terror mixed with excitement.

Bridezilla Murders

Deacon's cell phone rang, and he answered. It was Lynn. He told her where we were, and she said she'd meet us later since she had to go question the employees at Shelby's boutique. He played kissy face on the phone and hung up. I said they were about as disgusting as Penny and I were.

"Lynn said the city officials were hot to stop the Bridezilla killer or killers, that it didn't look good for the wedding industry here. She said she didn't need me, so I get to babysit your damn dog." He grinned widely.

"Well, truthfully, I'd rather be looking into the murder than chaperoning my family. But I have to be the good guy and entertain everyone. I know my mother will remember this trip for a long time. Tomorrow Penny and I get married, and then Sunday morning I put everyone on the jet back to Michigan. If Lynn doesn't tag the killer before that, maybe we can join in the fun."

"Sounds like a plan to me, but you get to carry the dog." Deacon laughed and roughed up Willy's head.

On the other side of town at Metro PD, a woman in a brown uniform with the logo Speedy Delivery on the back walked into the lobby with a package. The officer at the counter asked what she wanted; she said she had a delivery for Captain Weber. He said to leave it, but she replied that it had to be signed for by

Weber only. He paused, then picked up the phone and called Weber. A few minutes later he came out to the woman, asking for the package. She smiled and said she had a package for him, reached over and opened the front of the box. Inside was a small boombox, and she hit a button.

Music poured out as the woman pulled off her uniform, and Weber realized she was a stripper. The lobby went wild as all the officers came running over to watch as the stripper gyrated around Weber who was totally flustered. No one had noticed Trapper and Becker at the front door with a video camera taping the whole thing. Weber yelled for her to stop or he would have her arrested. She looked hurt and ran her hand down the side of his face saying he didn't like her. He flinched and stormed off to his office as the squad of cops cheered her on. He turned and yelled for everyone to get back to work and to go out and find Trapper, then vanished into his office. Everyone was still cheering the woman on as Trapper and Becker ran off to their rental car and got away, laughing their heads off.

Score two for the Vegas Jokers.

About a half hour later the copters flew back to the helipads, and out trooped my family. They were all raving about the sights and Mom was breathless. It was almost noon so we all piled into the van. I drove everyone to In-N-Out Burgers, and we had our lunch.

Bridezilla Murders

After eating, we went out to the huge mall north of town and wandered around there for a couple of hours. Penny finally gave the baby back as she was getting tired of carrying him. My son put the baby in a stroller and we continued.

I announced that we would be having dinner in the Stratosphere, the tallest structure west of the Mississippi and the place I almost took a dive off of. Then we were back in the van and on our way to dinner. This day was going fast, and I was glad. We got to the top of the Stratosphere and I had everyone seated right by the windows overlooking Las Vegas, a spectacular sight. The waiter arrived for ordering and we did so. While we waited for the food to come, I took Penny to the spot where I was pushed off the side of the building. She couldn't believe I held on for my life hanging so high off the ground. I told her I just thought of not being safely with her, that was how I held on.

Lynn called Deacon. He told her where we were, and she said she would join us, that she had enough playing detective on her day off. She arrived about a half hour later and told Deacon and me about her investigations. Nothing earthshaking, just routine stuff and no leads.

We all enjoyed the meal, finished and went back to the van. It was starting to get dark out so I drove everyone down the strip so we could admire the lights. I drove all the way down to the Luxor so they could see the beam of light shooting up, so powerful that it could be seen from space.

It was still early so we went to the Rio Hotel, and I took everyone in to see the Penn and Teller show. Luckily they still had some open seats. I hid Willy while we went by the ushers and sat rubbing his belly. That usually made him sleep.

The show was amazing and funny. We all were satisfied, and by this time everyone was worn out, much to my relief. I took them back to the hotel, and they all headed to their rooms. My son asked my mother if she could watch the baby for a while so he and his wife could go explore the strip. My son lived with me here for about five months until we went back to Michigan, so he knew his way around. I told everyone that the wedding was set for 1 P.M. tomorrow, and the van would be here to pick them up by noon.

They were all tucked safely away, so that left Deacon, Lynn, Penny and me to our own devices. We went back to the Bellagio, ordered room service, and sat talking about the Bridezilla case.

"I interviewed ten employees at Shelby's, eight women and two men," Lynn said. "They all had a hatred for Bridezillas, but I don't think enough to murder anyone. They all were a little wimpy to have done it. Neither of the murdered women had anything in common other than being bitches. If it were acceptable to kill the bitches, we'd have a lot less women in this world."

Penny said, "Amen to that. I've had a number of bitches on my show. I usually just blow them off by asking a few questions then going on to the next guest."

"The only person I suspected was this creepy guy who takes care of keeping the place clean. He was a bit off, kind of like the school geek who had the pocket protector and tape on his glasses. I grilled him a bit harder than the others, but he held on to his story." She was quiet for a few moments as if thinking about the whole thing. "I have no idea who may have done it, although I do believe that there were two killers involved. The way they were murdered, a gun and a knife, why not both vics murdered by the same weapon? Why the change? Must have been two different perps."

Penny looked at me. "Well, after we get hitched tomorrow and send off our relatives, we'll have more time to catch the killer."

I was a bit surprised that Penny was willing to investigate a crime rather than jump into bed for a few days. Maybe we were becoming an old married couple.

Lynn's cell phone rang. She answered and listened for a bit then said she was on her way. I could tell by her words that there was another murder. Deacon asked her what happened.

"It was Williams. He said a bride was coming out of Viva Vegas Wedding Chapel on the strip after she and her fiancé argued and she called off the wedding. The bride stormed around to the side of the building and was attacked and beaten just short of dead, saved by a tourist who saw the attack and yelled at the perp. He ran off, and the tourist called the police. She's alive but unresponsive; they think she'll be in a coma. Worst part, the wedding chapel said she was a customer of Shelby's."

Chapter 9

We all went to the Viva Vegas Wedding Chapel, and Williams made his crude remarks about how I was killing all the brides in Vegas. I looked at him and said he could be next. He toddled off after telling Lynn she could take the case. Lynn said he could just go home. CSI was checking the scene and surrounding areas while Lynn and Deacon talked to the chapel director. He said the bride, Cathy Ross, and the groom argued about the flower arrangement.

Then it got heated and she called off the wedding and stormed out.

"Who all was attending the ceremony?" Lynn inquired.

The director said just the mother and father of the groom. The bride's parents declined to come. They didn't like the groom.

"Aren't there any good weddings in Vegas, where everyone gets along?" I asked, knowing our wedding was going to be all right.

"Well, we have many weddings here in our chapel that go well, but occasionally there are the exceptions. There are many people who come here to get married for the wrong reasons, and they don't have the temperament to just get through it without fighting. Then there are the ones who don't really want to get married, so they pick and pick till the other says it's over. We get a lot of angry people here, which is sad as it should be a happy moment," the director replied to my comment.

"The bride and groom planned their wedding through Shelby Francis, is that correct?" Lynn asked.

"Yes, Shelby set up the whole affair for this bride and groom, but she didn't show up tonight to set it up. She sent her employees."

"Is that normal for Shelby?"

"Oh, yes, she arranges many weddings for us, but it's hard to be everywhere at once," he replied.

"Do you have surveillance cameras in the parking lot?"

"Of course, isn't Las Vegas one big surveillance camera nightmare?" He laughed.

She turned to Deacon and asked him to see if CSI had the tapes yet. He went off to find them.

"I want to see the tapes if they are still available," Lynn said.

The director said the tapes hadn't been taken yet, that he had them in his office. Lynn asked him to take us to them and called for Deacon to come back. We went to his office, and he ran the tape back to just before the attack. We watched as the bride came around the corner of the building and the assailant jumped out from the bushes, hitting her with a pipe. He kept hitting her as she fell. Penny looked away. I was about ready to look away myself just as the tourist, a big football quarterback type, came running up. He wasn't in time to tackle the assailant who ran off while the jock stopped to check on the bride. We saw him take out his cell phone, I presumed to call the cops. The tape kept going as people came running to the woman, and Lynn said to cut it off. She asked for the tape and gave it to a CSI standing by.

We all went back out to the scene of the crime and just stood until Lynn spoke.

"The tape doesn't really show if the assailant was a man or a woman, just someone in black clothes and a ski mask. Not much to go on. But how could the person know that there would be a bride coming around that side of the building? It's not likely that he or she just sat waiting for someone to come by, is it?"

"The assailant could have known the way the bride was, a Bridezilla, and figured she would pull this stunt. Maybe?" I offered.

"Sorry, Jim, it still doesn't make sense to me for the assailant to have been in the right place at the right time to commit the crime. OK, maybe this person had watched the couple carefully, knew where their car was, and figured the bride would travel that way if she did what was expected of her, call off the wedding. Maybe if she had gone through with the wedding, she'd be fine right now instead of in the hospital in a coma. Son of a bitch, I want this fucker."

CSI finished and Lynn questioned the jock. He didn't have much to say other than he saw the crime and stopped it. He was there for a friend's wedding and wanted to go to the reception. Lynn released him after getting his contact information. She grilled the groom and the bride's parents but got nothing more from them.

I suggested we go to Shelby's and see if someone might show up there. Lynn said it was better than standing around with our thumbs up our butts, so we went there. The building was dark, and Lynn and Deacon walked around the outside of it. Penny and I were standing out front, and as I was looking to the windows, I saw a light moving inside, like a flashlight. I called to Lynn as quietly as I could, and she came around the building. I pointed to the moving light and she said that was just cause for entering the building without a warrant. She asked Deacon to do the door. He crashed through it, and Lynn and Deacon went in. I had my Glock out and told Penny to stay behind me. She pushed Willy back into his purse and zipped it up.

I stopped in the reception room and told Penny we'd wait there for Lynn and Deacon. They went through the building, heard a crashing noise at the back of the building, glass breaking, and ran back there. They found a window in the back broken and someone running from the building. Lynn didn't want to risk anyone getting hurt in the neighborhood, so didn't fire her weapon. He was too far ahead to pursue anyway. They came back to us, and Lynn turned on the room light.

"The son of a bitch must have had a key to get in. No door or window was broken to get into the building, but they broke a window to get out when cornered in the back. I'll have CSI come by to see if he or she may have let some trace." She went off to make a call as we waited in the front of the building.

She came back and said, "Doesn't make sense. If the perp did work here, why the lights out and a flashlight? They could have just turned on the lights and lied saying they were here before we arrived."

"Maybe they don't work here and were looking for something, like a list of the Bridezillas who came here, if Shelby saved those?" I was guessing and everyone knew it.

"Good theory, but where did they get the key to get in?" Lynn asked.

"Former employee? Did you cover that with Shelby earlier?"

"No, it wasn't something that struck a chord. I'll be sure to ask that later," she said.

CSI arrived and Lynn showed them where to check. We stood out front as Shelby Francis drove up, having been called by Lynn.

"What happened? Was there another murder?" she asked, looking totally amazed.

"Shelby, I have to ask, where were you tonight from about 9 P.M. to now?" Lynn asked.

Shelby looked shocked and said "I've been at a party for my best friend. She was named director of child services at a clinic downtown. I was with about forty of my good friends." She answered but looked a bit annoyed.

"Sorry, but it's police protocol. There was a murder at the Viva Vegas Wedding Chapel, a woman named Cathy Ross. Did you know her?"

"Yes, she was in last week. We arranged her wedding early as she had business to attend to. Is she dead?"

"No, maybe in a coma. We'll know more later. Tell me, was she one of your Bridezillas?"

Shelby paused, and then said, "Well, she was difficult, gave her fiancé a hard time and pissed off her parents. They didn't like the groom. I made all the arrangements and then figured I wouldn't have anything to do with her after that day. I had my plans for tonight, so I sent one of my employees to be sure all went well. May I ask, if the murder was at the wedding chapel, why are you here?"

"We were checking out some leads. We saw someone in the building with a flashlight, an intruder or the murderer looking for more brides to kill, perhaps. The intruder ran and went out a back window when we entered the building," Lynn replied.

"Well, I'm sure the intruder wouldn't find any brides here after closing," Shelby said.

"Shelby, the intruder got in with a key. Do all your employees have keys?"

"Just the trusted ones and the supervisors. We also change the locks when someone quits, for security purposes."

"Well, that would leave out former employees." Lynn looked at me. "Shelby, do you keep any kind of file that list the difficult customers?" Lynn was pressing.

"Well, yes, I do list them, and put them in categories that we can use to identify the trouble makers before we agree to help them, but many slip past my criterion. I have the file in my office," she replied.

"May I see it, please?" Lynn asked politely.

"Of course, follow me." She went into the building to her office, over to a file cabinet and opened it. She dug around through the file folders and looked a bit stunned. She turned to us and said, "The file with the Bridezilla list is missing."

Chapter 10

"OK, Shelby, you're going to have to write down the names of the brides that still have weddings coming up. We are going to need protection for them." Lynn spoke firmly, probably pissed that there was a list to make it easy for the killer to pick and choose his victims.

Shelby went pale, sat at her desk, and took paper and pen to write the names. She checked with her desk calendar for the soonest upcoming ones and listed those first.

She looked up at us and said, "Why is my bridal salon being the target for the murders? There are plenty of others in town who are even bigger than I."

"The killer may have a connection to you, an employee or an angry former employee. For that matter, it may be a groom who went through your planning and is angry that his marriage didn't get started. God, who knows?" Lynn was sounding a bit frustrated. She looked at Penny and me and said, "I'm putting a couple of officers on your wedding tomorrow, just as a precaution." She said quietly to

Penny, "Not that you're a Bridezilla, but I'm not taking chances with you."

Penny thanked her and then felt Willy squirming in his bag. She'd forgotten to unzip the thing. Willy popped his head out and made a little yip at Penny. She apologized and nuzzled him.

Shelby finished and gave the list to Lynn who took it to one of her detectives standing outside the office. She told him to take some men to track down as many of these people as possible, starting with the weddings coming up the soonest, and see that they were protected.

"I'm putting everyone on this. I have the blessing of the city council to stop this killer before he puts a black spot on our wedding industry. I just want the fucker."

We all went out and discovered the camera crew was there taping as much as they could. I said, don't tell me, the police scanner. Lonie smiled and said, it comes in handy.

We were back at the Bellagio. It was almost midnight and we had a wedding to get through tomorrow. Lynn and Deacon said their good nights and said they'd be ready by 10 A.M. to help get us to the chapel. They left, and Penny and I sat on the couch looking out the window at Las Vegas. Again we were both a bit worn down and I just sat there with my arm around her.

"You still want to get married?" I smiled.

"Of course. I want to inherit all the money you have stashed away." She grinned and kissed my nose, which made Willy jump up and start licking both of us.

"Do you want to go and fool around as single people for one last time?" Penny asked, and I said I'd race her to the bedroom.

Willy got locked out of the bedroom for another night. He wasn't happy.

Saturday morning. It was a beautiful day, as it usually is in Las Vegas. The sun was beaming brightly, the sky was a sharp blue, and Penny was glowing. I kissed her, and we took Willy for his morning constitutional then ate breakfast. We got back to the room and found Lynn, Deacon and two uniformed officers at our door.

"Are we going into protective custody?" I asked.

Lynn smiled and said she was taking no chances with us. We went into the room, and I got my wedding outfit just as Buck and Maria came to the door. Buck saw the cops and looked a bit panicky. I explained the reason Penny was being escorted to the wedding, and he relaxed. I said I hadn't seen much of him the last few days, and he said that Maria was keeping him busy. He winked.

Deacon said he was going over to the MGM with the van to gather my family and take them to the chapel, as arranged. I thanked him, and he left. Lynn was going to be Penny's maid of honor, and they headed off with the cops to get Penny ready in her dress. Maria went with them to help, and I asked her to take charge of Willy for the wedding. She said she'd love to and took Willy and his bag. Buck and I were alone. He smiled and said good luck. I gave him a box, saying it's for the best man. He opened it and found a Rolex watch. He was speechless and put it on.

Buck and I left and got to the chapel around 11:45. We went into the groom's waiting room. Deacon came in and said everyone was in place. He explained to my family that the cops were friends who were invited. He also said the camera crew was doing their thing. I asked if Trapper and Becker had made it. Deacon said they were sitting quietly at the back of the chapel, probably to make a quick escape if the place was raided. He smiled. Deacon said that he put one of the two cops behind Trapper and Becker to be sure they didn't slip out.

Then Deacon laughed and said, "When Weber came in, I sat him next to Trapper. You should have seen Trapper and Becker sweat. Weber said he didn't want to upset the wedding, but he wanted to speak with Trapper after the ceremony."

I laughed at that and asked if the minister was ready. Deacon looked at me and asked if anyone told me that the wedding was being officiated by Elvis.

"Well, we got a problem. Penny can't stand Elvis. Go tell her now or she may become a Bridezilla when we go out."

Deacon went to the bride's room and told Lynn and Penny about Elvis. Shelby was there and thought Penny knew this was a chapel that had Elvis presiding.

"Shit, I'm not getting married by Elvis! I want a real minister, now. This wedding goes nowhere until this is changed." Penny had a look in her eyes that said don't mess with her wedding.

Shelby looked panicked and Lynn said to relax.

"OK, we can still save this. Let me make a call." Lynn went off to the side of the room and called someone, talked a bit, then made another call. She went back to Penny and Shelby.

"Penny, I have a friend, Reverend Mark, who is the pastor for a homeless mission off Fremont Street. He's ordained and licensed by the state to perform weddings. He said he'd be more than happy to do your wedding. I called for a cop car to pick him up and have him here ASAP. Will that do?"

"Are you sure he's OK?" Penny asked.

"Well, he presided over my marriage," Lynn responded.

"Lynn, you're a divorced woman now!" Penny was getting hysterical.

"Penny, Reverend Mark had nothing to do with my divorce. A slutty little blond did that." She laughed. Penny broke out in a laugh of relief, and Deacon said he would go tell me.

By 12:45 Reverend Mark had everyone's information and went to get ready for the ceremony. Guided by Shelby's assistant, Buck and I went out to the chapel. We stood in the chapel. I looked over my little gathering of family and friends along with the stage crew from the Flamingo and was a bit overwhelmed by it all. I had to smile when I saw Weber, Trapper and Becker all sitting quietly together at the back. I could imagine what was going through all their minds.

After a short time, the music started the bridal march, and Penny came out of the bride's room. She had asked Deacon to give her away, and he said he was honored to.

Bob Moats

I was stunned. She looked so beautiful, so amazingly beautiful, I wanted to cry. She got to me, and Deacon turned her over to me. I smiled at Deacon as he went to sit. Reverend Mark greeted everyone and said this was a moment of joy and a beginning. He did the little thing where he asked if there was anyone who felt this marriage should not take place. The room was silent, then Willy let out a tiny yip as Maria held him. Everyone laughed, and I said he didn't count. We gave our vows, said our I Dos, and exchanged rings, then Reverend Mark pronounced us husband and wife. I kissed the bride and turned to our family as Reverend Mark introduced us as Mr. and Mrs. Richards.

We went outside as the family threw bird seed. Penny insisted on that for the birds. We got into a Lincoln Limo I had reserved and had it drive us around Las Vegas. We kissed in the back and Penny asked if we could have sex back there. I said we should wait till we got back to our room.

We got to the MGM Grand Hotel and went into the banquet room where everyone was already seated and having their libations. Penny and I sat at the head table. Buck made a toast to us, then the food came. Shelby was making sure everything was going smoothly and had extra help along to be sure. Of course the camera crew was all over the place, taping everything for the show and our wedding memories.

Bridezilla Murders

Lynn had hired a local band with a great female singer that she personally knew. We all danced and partied until about 4 P.M. Then we opened up wedding gifts that we had told people not to give us, but you can't stop people from doing good. Penny and I went around and greeted Wally and Jamie and the guys from the stage crew, thanking them for coming. It made it a real Vegas wedding that way. My mother hugged Penny and welcomed her officially to the family. Penny scooped up the baby and danced with him on the dance floor. Alex's eyes went huge at the swirling they did. I asked the band to pause and thanked everyone for being with us old farts at our wedding. I said I hoped they would all enjoy our happiness and then I kissed Penny who came up with the baby.

I went to Reverend Mark, thanked him for coming on such short notice, and asked him about his homeless mission and how they were financed. He said they took mostly donations and had help from local churches for food and clothes. I took him to a table, wrote out a check, and gave it to him for his work. I said when I last lived here, I would see all the homeless people wandering the streets and it bothered me. I wanted to help but I wasn't able to, so I hoped the check helped and would try to send more when I could. He thanked me, said he had to get back to the mission and left.

A short while later Weber came up and thanked us for inviting him. He had no real family in town so it was a delight for him to be with us. Then he whispered to me, asking if I thought Trapper might be behind a few pranks in town. I said I didn't think so but you never could tell. He nodded and said he regretted having to leave but had to get back to work. After he left I said to Penny, that man just could not stay in one spot too long.

The reception wound down around 7 P.M. and everyone started to head out. I gathered my family and told them that I had arranged for them to stay in Vegas one more day till Monday. They could do what they wanted tomorrow. They were on their own. Penny and I would be busy, but we'd see them to the jet on Monday. I gave an envelope to my brother and one to my son and said this would help to make the extra day more pleasant. I said to spend it wisely and stay out of the casinos. I told everyone that my son knew the town so they could ask him for advice on what to do. They all were happy and went up to their rooms to change clothes.

Trapper and Becker came over, congratulated us again, and said they were going out to have a little more fun. I asked, "Does that involve red food coloring?" Trapper looked at me and said he didn't know what I was talking about, winked and was just leaving when Lynn said she would be watching him, that she heard about the stripper at the precinct. He laughed and said just try and catch him.

Chapter 11

Buck, Maria, Deacon and Lynn stood by us, Penny holding Willy, as I thanked them for everything they did to turn this into a beautiful day. They walked us out to the waiting limo just as Lynn's cell phone rang. I looked at her and said she was on her own, pulled Penny and Willy into the limo quickly, and had the driver take off for another ride around Vegas.

Lynn answered and listened, then hung up. She looked at Deacon and said the Bridezilla killer was escalating, that he just kidnapped a bride at a church over in North Las Vegas. They gave apologies to Buck and Maria and left to go to the church.

In another part of Vegas, in a dark garage, a woman in white was being dragged out of a car trunk. She was unconscious and a dark figure was pulling her to the basement stairs just off the garage. She was taken down the stairs, hitting her head on each step till she hit pavement. The dark figure pulled her to a cot in the middle of the room where her gown and under garments were removed and carefully hung up on the overhead floor joists by a hanger. The woman was tied down face up by her wrists and ankles to the cot, and the dark figure came over her, breathing heavily. She would never know the joy of her wedding day.

Lynn and Deacon arrived at the church and found the primary detective from North Las Vegas Police. Lynn knew him, Detective Lieutenant Max Kitter. He greeted Lynn and Deacon and said he called her since this was the same MO from her case.

"The perp is getting worse now. First a quick gun shot, then a risky knife stab, followed by a beating, now a kidnapping. If these weren't brides being killed, I'd say we had four different cases, but they are all brides. What's the name of the vic?" Lynn asked.

"She's Debbie Loraine, decided to have her wedding here because her groom is from Vegas. She and the groom had a falling out. She didn't like his choice of best man and he didn't like her bridesmaids. They fought and she ran out just before the wedding started. She was seen going out to the parking lot, but it's huge and unguarded with no security cameras. It was getting dark out, but a woman saw a person wrestle with what looked like a bride in white, hit her then put her in a trunk. The witness, a woman from the neighborhood, was frightened and didn't see much of the car before it sped away. She knows nothing about cars, just that it was black and beat up."

"Great, we're not catching a break," Lynn lamented. She pulled out her cell and dialed Shelby, waited then asked Shelby if she knew a Debbie Loraine. Shelby said she didn't know the woman and asked why. Lynn told her about the kidnapping and said this time it wasn't Shelby's salon involved. She thanked Shelby and hung up, telling Deacon and Kitter about what she said.

"Now I'm both wondering and worrying. If this has nothing to do with Shelby's Bridezillas, then we have a serial killer on our hands. Any Bridezilla is fair game. We need to send out a bulletin to all bridal planners, salons and boutiques." She thought about Penny. "I hope he only goes after unmarried brides."

Penny and I arrived back at our suite around 10 P.M. and fooled around while still in our wedding clothes. Willy was locked out of the bedroom again and sat by the door waiting for us. He had a long wait.

Sunday morning, it was beautiful again. I called my brother and asked what they had planned. He told me what they were going to do, and I said that was good and to keep in touch. I hung up just as Penny came up behind me and put her arms around my expansive waist. She whispered that she had a talk with Eric and said he could no longer visit her in her dreams, they were only meant for me, her husband. I said I gave up Pixie the moment I saw Penny come down the aisle. We both laughed, and I turned to her to search for her tonsils.

My cell phone rang. It said Deacon. I looked at Penny and asked if we should answer it. She said if we don't they'll just bust down our door. I picked it up and answered.

"Can't you let us married people rest?" I said.

"You can rest when you get back to Michigan. Right now Lynn needs your expert opinions. She gets a little unsure of herself sometimes, and I didn't tell her I was calling you. I can tell her you called me to see how we were doing, I told you about the new case we got of a kidnapped bride, and you said you were coming down to stick your nose into it." He laughed.

"Well, if I do that I'll have something to hold over your head. Where are you?"

He told me and I said we'd be there. Penny could hear the conversation on my phone, and when I hung up she jumped up and headed to the bedroom. I asked where she was going. She said to get dressed, we had a case to solve. We dressed, picked up Willy and went out.

We got to Metro PD and went into Lynn's office. She asked how our first night of wedded bliss was. I said a little better than connubial bliss for most people. Penny said it was adequate. I just gave her a dirty look.

"OK, we're ready to go. What have you got so far?" I asked.

Lynn sighed. "We got squat. The witness at the kidnapping only saw a black beat-up car. It headed east in the direction of the mountains, the witness said. I would have the mountains combed, but I don't have enough people to go traipsing on a wild goose chase. CSI said the person in the beating video was, based on the height of the bride, about five nine or ten. Slight build and no other remarkable features. The employees at Shelby's finally admitted they were staying away from the first Bridezilla so they weren't around when someone opened the door and shot her."

"Did the kidnapped bride have a purse?" I asked.

Lynn looked at the statements of the people from the wedding and said, "One of the bridesmaids saw her pick up her purse when she stormed out. It was not found in the parking lot. Why?"

"Maybe she has a cell phone and maybe it has GPS tracking."

Lynn just said crap and picked up her phone. She got hold of the CSI supervisor and asked if it was possible to track the vic's cell phone. He said they'd get on it. Lynn took us down to the crime lab and into the electronic wizard's domain. The supervisor greeted us and said he had his people check with the family about her cell phone and got the phone number. They ran a check to see if it was GPS enabled. The tech sitting at the computer said he checked with Verizon, and she did have an active tracker. He punched a bunch of keys on his computer and hacked into the phone company towers. A map came up of North Las Vegas and a couple of lines coordinated together to land at an address on Wheat Street. The tech pulled up an address and gave it to the supervisor. He gave it to Lynn, and she ran out.

We followed her back to the squad room. She was yelling that there might be a break in the kidnapping. She got on the phone, called the DA to get a warrant and said to get it ASAP, the bride might not be dead yet. She gathered up her people and called for SWAT. She was coordinating when her phone rang. She had the warrant. She yelled, let's roll!

We all drove out to the address. It was a rundown house in a slum area of North Vegas, the kind of place that tourists don't see unless they take a wrong turn off the strip. Everyone rolled up to the house, frightening neighbors who sat on their porches trying to cool themselves in the heat of the afternoon. Lynn and Deacon went to the garage and looked in. The glass was painted over but there was a small scraping in one corner. Lynn peeked through and saw a beat-up black Buick. She signaled the rest of the officers, and they went to the side door of the house and smashed it in with the battering ram. The SWAT team streamed in and found the place clear. I insisted Penny and Willy stay in the car until there were results. I told her to lock the doors. She did. I went to the garage and looked in. Lynn, Deacon and the captain of the SWAT team were tearing into the car. They got the trunk opened and found the bride's purse complete with cell phone. Lynn looked at me and gave me a nod.

Lynn yelled to everyone to fan out and find the bride, look for hidden rooms if possible. I went to the side of the garage and saw the door in the floor. I called Lynn and she came over. She called for back-up, and they opened the door then carefully went down into the dark and smelly basement with two SWAT officers leading the way.

Lynn found a switch on the wall by the stairs and flicked it on. The room was flooded with light from just about everywhere. It lit up like daylight. Everyone turned to the center of the room where they saw the cut up body of the bride.

Chapter 12

Trapper and Becker strolled down the Boulevard and came to the bike stand where the Metro PD bicycle cops parked their bikes. The cops were in the coffee house getting their lattes and donuts. Trapper took one end of the bike cable and Becker took the other end, stretched it out and through the bike tires, then locked the ends around the bike rack. Trapper went up to the window of the coffee shop and tapped on the glass. The cops turned to see Trapper give them a smile and the finger. They all jumped up and stormed out to their bikes as Trapper and Becker headed up the strip. Then they stopped and turned to watch the cops pull their bikes from the rack only to collide and stumble around with the secured bikes. Trapper videotaped the whole incident, and then the two of them ran off.

The cops were pissed but then a couple of them started to laugh. They found that the key was still in the lock so they could get their bikes free. One cop found a playing card of the Joker, the one the late Heath Ledger portrayed, on his radio and laughed his head off.

Score three for the Vegas jokers.

Bridezilla Murders

CSI and the ME were doing their best to find evidence as to the identity of the killer. The owner of the house was called and came in to tell Lynn that the house was rented by phone. The person sent a money order before moving in. He never met the man, was told the man was from out of town and wanted a place to land easily. It was a furnished house and ready to occupy. Lynn asked the landlord why he didn't check his references. He said he had enough problems trying to rent the place since it was a bad neighborhood, so why rock the boat.

A CSI officer came out to tell Lynn that his guy must have worn gloves the whole time he lived there. It was clean of prints. Lynn asked if the landlord had a copy of the money order. He said he did and would get it to her. He regretted renting to the man now that he committed a murder in the place. That would make it real hard to rent. Lynn looked at him and said she felt so sorry for him, then she quietly called him an asshole when he walked out of the garage.

The ME removed the body of the bride, and CSI had the wedding gown bagged and ready to go to the lab for examination. Lynn, Deacon and I wandered through the house. I could see Penny and Willy standing out front by the porch. She saw me through the window and waved.

"The house doesn't look very lived in, no clothes or personal items, almost as if he used it as a front or just a place to bring the girl. But he could have rented a motel room and done the deed. This guy is not making sense," Lynn commented, mostly to herself.

We tore apart the place and found nothing of importance in identifying the killer. The car was examined by CSI, and they told Lynn there were no prints in the car either and that it was reported stolen days ago from down in Henderson. Lynn asked if they checked the bathroom for hair in the shower or anything to take DNA from. They told her they found traces of hair in the drain but it looked like it had been there for a while, probably from prior tenants. Otherwise it was clean.

Lynn hoped there would be some trace on the wedding gown from the perp, a hair or a print, anything to get a fix on him. I went out to keep Penny company, and we waited for Lynn and Deacon to finish. They came out, and Lynn was not smiling. She thanked me for the mention about the cell phone. They would have never had found her right off. Unfortunately, it was too late to save her.

CSI finished and Lynn had the remaining officers seal up the place, then the four of us went to find somewhere to get a late lunch. We sat at Del Taco eating and talking about the wedding, trying to get our minds off the murders for a while. Lynn said she loved watching Trapper trying to avoid Weber at the reception. She said Trapper was good at evading him. I said he was good at evading police work, too. He spent a lot of time at my office hiding from his job, waiting for his retirement. Deacon said he started hiding out when he became a lieutenant. He would assign people jobs then vanish. I said I hoped Becker didn't pick up his bad habits.

Penny thanked Lynn for bringing in Reverend Mark. She said she liked his demeanor and his presentation. I looked at her and asked what college she attended. Lynn said that Reverend Mark stopped her just before he left and thanked her for calling him. He said Jim made a very generous contribution to the mission.

Penny looked at me and said, "If you keep giving your money away to everyone, I'll have nothing to inherit when you keel over." I kissed her and said I had a small fortune stashed away for just that occasion. What I didn't tell her was I took out a huge life insurance policy. I was surprised they gave it to me with me being in such a hazardous occupation. I was worth over a million dollars to Penny if I keeled over. I wasn't going to tell her. She might get ideas.

She looked at me and asked, "By the way, do you have any life insurance on you?"

"I have a small policy, not worth killing me over." I smiled and wondered if she read my mind.

"Well, it better be enough to take care of me in my old age after you're gone."

"It will be. Now can we get off my death? It's creeping me out," I insisted.

We finished our tacos, nachos, burritos and salsa dip and went out to the parking lot. I said I was feeling gaseous. Penny said to expel the gases before we got in the car. I said it would be a few minutes.

"So Lynn, what's the plan of attack now?" I asked as we expelled our gases in the lot.

"I'm hoping that the lab finds something of value. Right now, I'm going to visit the wedding planner who set up Debbie Loraine's wedding and see if she has had any strange things happening. Care to come along?"

I looked at Penny, and she said, "Onward and upward."

We all headed to the Weddings by Design Studio just off Charleston Avenue and went in to the receptionist. Lynn flashed her badge and asked for the head person. The receptionist made a quick call and a woman of about fifty, blond and well-built, came out and introduced herself as Wendy Darling. We just stared as she said, "It was a joke by my parents. Now please ask me where Peter Pan is and we can get on with the interrogation." She didn't sound like a happy Wendy.

Bridezilla Murders

"We're not here to interrogate you, Miss Darling. Is there a private place we can go to talk?" Lynn asked. Wendy Darling looked at the four of us and the dog and asked if the dog was a police dog. I said he was a bloodhound. She cracked a smile and asked us to follow her.

We went to what looked like a conference room and sat around the big circular table. Lynn sat next to Wendy who asked Penny to sit next to her so she could pet Willy. He loved that.

"I'm sure by now you know of the kidnapping of Debbie Loraine. We found her this morning. She was murdered." Wendy looked faint as Lynn continued. "Can you tell us anything that may help our investigation? What was she like to work with?"

"She was a bitch, simple as that. I could tell her stupid family was going through the motions just to please her, but she wouldn't be pleased. I'm surprised they even made it to the church."

"OK, you get Bridezillas often, I presume?" Lynn asked.

"Oh, sure, they're part of the fabric of weddings. Every woman is commander of her moment and don't mess with her plans. Some are just worse than others. Sure we get a lot of good ones, but in the summer when the Vegas temperatures are up, so is the temperature of the brides. I like winter weddings better."

"Can you tell me anything about Debbie, her family and the groom?"

"Well, as I said, they were all goofy, not enough of a brain in the entire lot combined to fill the head of a frog. I could see Debbie was the ringleader, and she hated the groom's best man. The groom wasn't pleased with the bridesmaids either."

"Was anyone else hanging around the wedding party that seemed out of place?"

"There was this one young man. He had a smitten look on his face whenever Debbie went by. I assumed he was with the wedding party, but when I asked him if he was here to be fitted for a tux, he said he wasn't in the wedding party and left rather quickly and rudely."

Lynn perked up and asked about how tall he was. Wendy replied about her height, five-ten.

Lynn asked if she would be willing to look at some mug books and see if he could be in any of them. She said she would give an hour of her time in the morning, she had an opening then. Lynn thanked her and we went to leave. Wendy asked Penny what the dog's name was. She said Willy. Wendy patted Willy's head and said she'd see us in the morning.

Chapter 13

Before we left the conference room, Lynn asked if Wendy kept track of the Bridezillas in a file or list. She said no, but she did note the problem brides in their individual files. Lynn asked where she kept those files. Wendy told her in her office under lock and key.

Lynn asked if she could have a list of upcoming weddings that had problem brides in them; Wendy said sure and went to her office. She went to the file cabinet to get out her files on upcoming weddings, but was amazed that the cabinet was not locked. Lynn asked her not to touch the cabinet further and went to look at it carefully. She noted that the lock catches had been bent back. Someone forcibly opened the cabinet.

Lynn got on her cell phone and requested a CSI team to come dust for prints on a file cabinet. She hung up and asked Wendy if she had seen the same strange man from Debbie's group hanging around the place. Wendy said if he had been there, she would have called the police. Lynn carefully opened the cabinet so as not to disturb any prints and asked Wendy to look in, but not touch, files to see if they were all there. Wendy looked at the tabs on the file folders and said that they were out of order, not the way she would place them. She took a breath and said someone had messed with her files.

About an hour later the CSI team had dusted just about everything within the vicinity of the file cabinet. Wendy volunteered her prints, and CSI used a new device that recorded finger prints on a portable scanning platform. No ink involved. This would clear Wendy's prints from the unauthorized ones on the cabinet and folders. The forensic scientists did their work and left to go examine the findings. Lynn was hoping for a good print, but from the house experience, it wasn't a good bet.

Lynn asked again for a list of upcoming weddings that might have a high risk for attack. Wendy went through the now released folders, saying she could tell which ones were disturbed, and wrote out the names from those files, giving it to Lynn.

We all left the building and went out to the parking lot. Lynn said she would get her people on these weddings. I asked to see the list. Lynn handed it to me. I read down the names and stopped at one.

"OK, this may be way out in left field to use an old cliché, but I noticed the names of the previously murdered or attacked brides were, so far, alphabetical. First was Annamarie, then Becky, then Cindy and last, Debbie. I may be wrong, but the only bride on this list that starts with an "E" is Edith Goring. Wouldn't hurt to check her out. Her wedding is tonight."

Before she could say anything her cell phone buzzed. She answered and listened, then hung up.

"Well, interesting. CSI said they took the cot Debbie was tied to and when they removed the blanket wrapped around it, there was big writing on the cot from a paint marker. It said 'if you won't marry me, you won't marry anyone.' They also said they found a couple of hairs on the dress, but they couldn't get a match to anyone in the DNA database. This guy is off the records or never been hauled in. The cot did have a price tag on it from Park Surplus over off Martin Luther King Boulevard. We can check it later, but first I think we should have a talk with Edith Goring. Shall we take a ride?"

We all got into my SUV and drove to the address Wendy had supplied of the hotel that Edith was staying at. We drove into the Hilton Hotel parking and then went to the reception desk. Lynn flashed her badge and asked for Edith Goring's room number. The girl at the counter turned to the manager standing nearby and told him what Lynn asked for. It's not policy to give out room numbers, but in the case of the law it is an exception. The girl was being cautious. The manager checked Lynn's ID closely and said anyone could flash a plastic badge, but he was satisfied with Lynn's credentials. He looked up the room number and gave it to us, then we headed to the elevators.

We arrived at the fifth floor and went down the long hallway, spotting the room number. As we came to the door we heard crashing and screaming. Lynn pounded on the door yelling that she was the police and to open up. There was more crashing. Lynn knew the door wouldn't break open even if Deacon hit it. I saw a maid coming out of a room down the hall. Lynn saw her too and ran down, grabbing her arm and pulling her to the door in question. She showed her badge and said to open it. The frightened maid pulled a room card out and inserted it in the door lock. Lynn opened the door, then she and Deacon carefully went in with guns drawn. I held Penny and Willy back until I knew the situation.

I stood at the door as I heard Deacon yell, "Put down the lamp, lady!" I was a bit surprised by the comment and stepped into the room with my Glock in hand. I saw a half crazed woman standing in the center of the room holding a table lamp above her head as though she would throw it at Deacon. She stopped as soon as she saw his gun and got wide eyed, lowering the lamp.

Deacon ran around, pulled the lamp from her hand, and tossed it aside. Lynn came up after checking around to see if the woman was alone and got in her face. "What is your problem?" Lynn yelled.

The woman dropped to the floor sobbing loudly, leaving Deacon and Lynn standing in shock. Lynn bent down and said, a little calmer now, "Are you Edith Goring?" The woman nodded affirmatively between sobs. She looked miserable in a worn robe that had many miles on it. Lynn asked Deacon to help her up to the couch. He reached down and helped lift her gently by her arm to the overstuffed couch next to them. She sat back and started to weep loudly. I wondered if she was jilted or she ended her marriage. I presumed her grief was because of the wedding.

Lynn finally broke through Edith's sobs. "Edith, what's wrong?"

Edith looked at Lynn. Her mascara was running making her look like a wretched version of Alice Cooper. She tried to speak but this high-pitched, whiny, nasal sound came out of her mouth, unintelligible words mouthed between deep breaths.

"Edith, get hold of yourself. Relax, please, and just talk to me," Lynn begged.

Edith finally said something understandable. "Larry threatened to leave me!" She wailed loudly again, causing Lynn to step back.

Penny was standing at the door taking this all in, then she came forward to Edith and sat next to her. She pulled Edith to her and patted her like a baby saying, "There, there, I understand what you're going through."

Edith took a deep breath and said, "You do?"

"I most certainly do. I've had men threaten to leave me, too." Penny consoled the woman.

Edith drew back and looked at Penny, nodding her head. "Men are all bastards." She turned to Lynn and said quietly, "I gave that man the best year of my life. I did everything for him, made his food, cleaned his house, and then he tells me I'm miserable to live with. He called off the wedding." She started wailing again, this time plopping on Penny's lap almost crushing Willy who was still in his bag. Willy yelped, and the woman looked startled. Then, seeing Willy, she got all mushy, talking to him like he was a baby.

Lynn pulled Edith away from Willy and asked her where she was from. Edith answered that she was from Mississippi, Tupelo to be exact. I started picturing her clan of hillbillies all waiting at the church for her. She said Larry and she came out to get married and he started drinking and gambling, then he got mean with her. I wondered if there were groomzillas.

Bridezilla Murders

Lynn looked around the room. There were a couple of broken lamps. Otherwise not much else was damaged. Just as Lynn was going to ask Edith another question, a man came storming in the room. Judging from his torn jeans and a t-shirt that said, 'I Love Las Vegas,' I presumed he was Larry.

"Edith, who are these people?" he demanded.

Lynn came up fast in his face, putting her badge to his nose and saying, "We're the police! Who are you?"

He got a panicked look on his face, and stammered, "I'm Edith's fiancé. What's going on here?"

Edith jumped up and snatched at Lynn's gun in its holster. Lynn grabbed her arm and twisted before Edith could get hold of the weapon. "Hey, that's a no-no," Lynn yelled at Edith.

Edith pointed at Larry and cried, "I want this man arrested. He raped me!"

Chapter 14

"Rape!" Larry looked really panicky now. "I didn't rape no one, least of all this whore. She begged me for it. Bitch!" he yelled at Edith. Lynn grabbed Larry's arm and pulled him away from Edith. Deacon came around and latched onto him, taking the squirming Lothario away from them. Deacon handcuffed Larry as he protested, "Edith, they're going to arrest me. How can you do that to me?"

Edith looked shocked that Deacon had handcuffed Larry and wailed, "Don't take him away. He done nothing wrong. I was just mad at him."

Deacon grinned at Lynn as she suppressed her own grin. Edith ran to Larry, threw her arms around him, and apologized to him, asking Deacon to let him loose. Deacon looked at Lynn and she nodded. He uncuffed Larry, and the two lovebirds billed and cooed till it got sickening. Lynn came to Edith and asked her if she was still getting married. Edith turned to Larry and he said of course they were getting hitched. Edith jumped all over him and said she had to get ready.

Bridezilla Murders

"Edith, Larry, I have to inform you of a few things first," Lynn said, looking at Edith. "Your life may be in danger." The lovebirds looked shocked as Lynn explained about the murders of former brides, not specifically calling them Bridezillas, but just that Lynn believed that Edith might need protection. She asked if the couple would care if Lynn put police around their church, undercover so it would not bother the wedding guests, but they would be there to stop any attempts on her life. They both agreed and Lynn said to go get ready, then she asked how they were going to the chapel. Larry said in his 1968 Chevy Nova. I laughed silently since I had one myself years ago and could imagine the condition of Larry's car. Lynn said they had a real nice unmarked Crown Victoria police vehicle that they could use with an officer chauffeuring them. Larry looked a little distressed, probably from the police being in such close proximity to his family, but they agreed.

Lynn made a couple calls and said that it was arranged. When the officers arrived, Lynn said we were going to check out the church and would call them with any information they might need. We left the hotel and drove over to Holy Redeemer Church and into the lot. We walked around the perimeter of the building, and then Lynn had a few more undercover officers to watch the building. We went in as the unmarked Crown Vic drove up and deposited the bride and groom, looking much better than they did earlier.

Bob Moats

I was wrong about the hillbillies in the church. They all looked very respectable, and I found out that Larry was from Boulder City, south of Vegas, so the family didn't have far to travel. Edith had no family, so she wasn't represented by relatives. Penny and I sat on the bride's side along with Lynn and Deacon, alone. I felt sorry for Edith for some odd reason, I guess thinking about my family being in town for my wedding to Penny and Edith having no one close to celebrate her joy.

The wedding started without a hitch and moved along smoothly. I was waiting for Edith to break out and call it off, but she held to the end. They went out of the church with everyone throwing the traditional rice, much to Penny's dismay. She would have rather they threw bird seed. Edith and Larry looked completely happy as they went to the Crown Vic and got in the back seat. Lynn leaned toward me and said that either the killer didn't plan on using this bride, or we frightened him off.

Deacon was watching the driver of the Crown Vic and asked Lynn if that was one of her men. Lynn looked at the driver as he was pulling away. She got on her cell phone and called Detective Warren who was assigned to the detail and asked who was driving the car. Warren replied that Baker was given the car detail. Lynn went cold and said to get all cars to pursue the Crown Vic, the driver wasn't Baker. It must be the Killer.

Bridezilla Murders

"Son of a bitch, the killer grabbed both of them, right in front of us and with our own car! This is pissing me off!" Lynn screamed, scaring a couple of guests nearby.

The wedding guests were a bit shocked to see three police cars come from out of the side streets, flashers and sirens blaring. One car pulled up to the church, and Lynn and Deacon got in. I held Penny back as we couldn't go on a car chase. We returned to our SUV and drove out, heading in the general direction of the chase. I had my window down so I could hear the sirens.

Lynn was pounding on the dashboard, swearing like a sailor. Deacon was in back holding on for dear life as the officer driving was in hot pursuit. "I want this bastard, and I want those kids safely back to enjoy their wedding. Son of a bitch, move it, Jasper. Catch up to them."

Lynn called for every car in Vegas to pursue the Crown Vic and to proceed with caution, so as not to harm the two people in the back. She said everyone had her permission to shoot the son of a bitch driver. She retracted that comment and said to just wound him, she wanted his ass.

I was driving east on Cheyenne Avenue as I saw the camera crew van come barreling from up a side street. I couldn't believe it as the driver waved to me. Penny said the crew was part of her station's news team, so they were used to following the scanner and getting into the thick of a story. I actually laughed under the circumstances. At least I could follow them; they had the police scanner. The van went onto U.S. 95, so I followed heading south. I was thinking about the car chase down this same freeway system, chasing the criminal Wallace just before he crashed his car, last time we were in Vegas. I hoped for a less harmful fate for the newlyweds.

Lynn was listening to the scanner giving updates as to the location of the fleeing Crown Vic. They were traveling onto I-515 heading south towards Henderson. Lynn took count. There were about eight cars in pursuit, but the Crown Vic had the police interceptor package and it was fast. Two more cars joined ahead of the Crown Vic and tried to block it without causing accidents to other cars on the freeway.

The killer finally must have realized he was in trouble, so he turned off the side of the freeway going up an embankment and into a field behind a factory. The rest of the police cars followed up the hill and saw that he was in a box situation. The killer crashed a gate and was trying to go down a side street just as the camera crew van was coming from the other direction, followed by us. The van driver must have been slightly insane as he headed straight for the car, veering off at the last moment as the Crown Vic turned into a backyard of someone's home and came to a crashing halt against a brick BBQ. All the pursuers pulled up to the opening in the wood privacy fence that was torn apart by the car, and everyone streamed to the yard with guns out.

They ran up to the car ready to fire on the killer but found the driver seat was empty. The newlyweds in the back were screaming to be let out. Lynn opened the back door and they climbed out. Larry was storming around saying he couldn't get his hands on the nut job because of the metal mesh that separated the back from the front. Edith just looked totally frazzled. The camera crew was taping everything, and I came up to see Lynn having a fit because the killer got away. She screamed for everyone to search the vicinity and don't come back without his head. She told one of her detectives to take the newlyweds to their reception, watch them carefully, then take them back to the Hilton Hotel, treat them to a great dinner and get them put in the honeymoon suite on the Metro PD then to put a watch on them since they knew what the killer looked like up close. They were shocked and overjoyed. They left thanking Lynn and looking better than they did a few minutes ago.

I went to Lonie and asked her how she knew to take that road along the freeway. She said lots of experience, a scanner and a map of the city. I said I wanted a copy of their tapes for my memory box. She said she'd get it to Penny for me, then she went off to direct the camera man. Lynn came over to Penny and me and looked the worst I had seen her since I first met her on our last trip here. Deacon went off into the neighborhood to ferret out the killer, but I felt he was long gone.

"I'm happy the newlyweds are OK. We will get this asshole." Lynn sat down on a lawn chair in the yard. By now the owners of the house had gotten up the courage to come out after seeing all the cops. Lynn apologized for the condition of the yard but said she was sure their insurance would cover something like a police chase and crash into the BBQ.

Chapter 15

Her team returned after forty-five minutes of canvassing the area, no killer found. Deacon said they turned over every rock in the neighborhood. Lynn wasn't happy, but she took solace that one woman was safe now. She looked at the list Wendy gave her, and there was no bride with a name starting with an "F." I suggested she check with other wedding planners to see if they had any break-ins or files messed with. She called Detective Warren over and explained the plan. He rushed off taking a good portion of the men with him. Lynn said they found Baker, the real driver. He was unconscious next to the church, but he'd be all right. His ego was bruised worse than his head.

Bridezilla Murders

My cell phone rang. It was my brother telling me how good a day they had and asking if they would see Penny and me before the night was over. I looked at Penny and said we'd come by around eight and visit with them. I hung up and looked at my watch. It was just before seven. I told Lynn that we had enough crime fighting for the night and invited them to the MGM to visit with our family. Lynn said she'd see, but they probably would stop by our suite later to unwind. She didn't think the killer would screw around anymore tonight.

I called Buck and asked what they were up to. He said they were at the Boulevard Mall walking around window shopping. I invited him to visit with us and my family at the hotel; he said they'd be there by eight.

I looked at Lonie and her crew and asked if they had enough footage for the day. She smiled and replied that they did and went to pack it in. Penny and I headed back to the SUV after Lynn said they would go to Metro in a patrol car.

Penny, Willy and I traveled south to the MGM Grand and up to my brother's suite where we found him and his wife, my son and family and Mom relaxing. Penny gave Willy to me, kidnapped our grandson, and went off to the couch to talk his ear off. The family excitedly related their day to us, and I called for room service. Buck and Maria arrived, and shortly afterward Lynn and Deacon popped in. I was surprised. Lynn said they had enough of murder for one day. We all sat around and had our refreshments brought quickly by waiters all waiting for a handsome tip. I obliged.

I was sitting on the couch holding a very relaxed Willy, petting his belly and feeling good being with family and friends and my new bride who, forty-some years ago, was a very cute little cheerleader and the object of a number of my teenage dreams. I sat back taking it all in and enjoying the moment.

Lynn's cell phone rang and she sat looking at it, hesitating, then answered. She listened for a full minute then started laughing out loud. Everyone looked at the crazy woman laughing hysterically. She got up, went to the bathroom, and then came out a couple minutes later. Penny, Deacon, Maria, Buck and I were standing by the door waiting to see what news she had. She looked at us and started laughing again, then calmed down and told us that Warren heard what Trapper and Becker had done today and had to call.

"Well, it seems a company sign truck pulled up to the front of the Riviera Casino and the sky lift took two men up to the banks of lights making up the marquee out front. Security came out and was told they were there to replace the light bulbs. They worked for a while then left. About an hour ago when it got dark those lights went on. The casino was told that there were a number of bulbs out and the darkened bulbs spelled out the words across the front of the building, "WEBER IS A WUSS".

Score four for the Vegas jokers.

Around eleven my mom begged off and went to her room. My son and his wife decided to pack it in, too. I told them all to be ready in the morning to go back to the jet for the return trip to Michigan. I asked Lynn, Deacon, Buck and Maria if they wanted to join us at our suite, and we all headed down there, leaving my brother and his wife to hit the sheets.

At our suite I called their room service and got refreshments and snacks and we relaxed. Around midnight Penny's cell phone rang for the first time since we got to Vegas. She looked worried and checked the caller ID. It was her producer. She went off to the side of the room and talked for about a half hour, then finished.

"I don't believe it. Gordy, my producer, called and said he talked to Lonie about all the footage they got of the wedding and the extra footage they got of the murder investigation. He said if we solved the case before we were scheduled to return next Thursday, the station would pay for our entire trip out here, rooms, cars and all of it. Just for the rights to run the thing on my show or a special show just about the crime."

Lynn said, "I may not sign off on using my image unless I get some compensation." She giggled, and I said we could bill it to the station.

I was overjoyed that they would pay for everything. I wasn't poor, but this would keep my bank balance looking good. I turned to Lynn and said we were going to find this guy before next Thursday or I would never speak to her again. She laughed and said promises, promises.

We talked for a while longer, then everyone said it was time to be heading out. They all left and Penny and I sat on the couch going over the day. We headed to the bedroom before Willy figured where we were going; he was shut out again and was not happy about it.

Monday morning brought a new day and we were getting ready to send our family off to Michigan. Deacon arrived with the van, saying Lynn had to go in to work. We drove over to the MGM Grand for one last time and saw the folks standing by the guest pick-up. The camera crew was there documenting the departure. I smiled at Lonie and thanked her for telling Gordy about the footage. She said her pleasure; she wanted the scoop.

I asked my brother if they had checked out. He said that they did and handed me the billing printout. I looked at it and felt more determined to find the killer.

I asked where Trapper and Becker were. My brother handed me a note, and I read it with Deacon looking over my shoulder. It basically said that Trapper and Becker had checked out of the MGM and went to a motel off the strip, got a room till Thursday and asked if they could hitch a ride back when we went to Michigan. He said they could get a commercial flight if not. I laughed and looked at Deacon. "Trapper hasn't totally destroyed Vegas yet, so he's sticking around."

"Yes, and he didn't say what motel he was at either. He's hiding out." Deacon grinned.

We packed everyone into the van. Buck and Maria hadn't shown up since Buck was staying till Penny and I went back. We headed to McCarran Airport and to the business terminals, spotting the company jet waiting for us. The same pilots and flight attendant greeted us, and I helped get my family safely aboard. I told my brother that a limo would be waiting for them to go back to our house where they left their cars. Penny and I hugged and kissed everyone. Penny asked if she could keep the baby with us. I said no. The jet closed up and was getting ready to taxi out to the runway. We waved to everyone looking out the windows, and I felt a little sad. We hadn't spent very much time with everyone the last five days, but at least they enjoyed their stay.

The jet moved out and took off into the blue, leaving Las Vegas. Penny had a tear in her eye. I kissed it and said, "Don't be sad, Mrs. Richards."

"That's Mrs. Wickens-Richards to you." She smiled and kissed me. "But Penny Richards sounds nice. I may just change it and tell my producer to change the credits on my show."

"I think you should leave it at Wickens, or people won't recognize you," I offered. She said she'd think about it and kissed me again.

Deacon asked if we were done sucking face and said he had to get the van back to the rental place. I said hopefully the station would be paying for it, and we departed the airport.

We took the van back after I got the SUV to pick up Deacon at the car rental, and we went to Metro PD. Deacon took us in the back way. We went directly to Lynn's office. She was on the phone, but she waved to us and motioned to sit. We did just as Weber was coming down the hallway. I wanted to hide but he spotted us. Lynn just finished her call as Weber came in.

"May I ask if Trapper is still with your little group?" he said rather calmly. That worried me.

I said that my family had left Vegas this morning to return to Michigan. He asked if that included Trapper. I said that he didn't make it to the flight. He smiled and said that meant Trapper was still in town, good. He went out, and I said that was scary. I felt sorry for Trapper if Weber got hold of him. Lynn laughed and said that Weber heard about the Riviera lights thing this morning and he just went pale and said nothing. Everyone thought he was having a stroke, but he smiled and went to his office.

I thought Weber was plotting something. I should warn Trapper.

Chapter 16

"OK, on to our criminal. Where are we at with the Bridezilla killer?" I asked hoping they were hot on his trail. Lynn laughed and said they were no further today than they were yesterday.

"Wendy Darling was in and went through the mug books, found no one who matched the creep she had in her boutique. I had a sketch artist work with her and came up with this." She handed us the picture, but Lynn said it didn't match the man they saw driving the Crown Vic from the church. They had Edith and Larry look at it, and they said it wasn't him.

"Edith and Larry came in early this morning to work with the sketch artist but argued so much they had to be separated. Each gave their individual versions of the guy. Neither picture looked alike so we still don't have a good sketch of him," Lynn lamented. "I said that Edith's picture looked more like the guy I saw at a distance, but it wasn't conclusive."

Warren poked his head in the door and said they tracked down every wedding planner in Vegas and had a list of all the brides, alphabetized and listed as to the closest ceremonies coming up. He said the "F" category had two weddings, both today. Lynn said to get two sets of undercover men on it and took the list that Warren had. She looked at it and handed it to me. I perused the names and noticed that one of the women getting married today came from Mississippi. Odd I thought, so did Edith. I asked Lynn if she could check and see where the first three brides came from. She opened the file she had started for the murders and studied it a bit then said quietly, son of a bitch, they all came from Mississippi.

"What are the odds that they all came from the same state? About a zillion to one," I observed.

Lynn thought for a minute and said, "The killer wrote on the cot that if the bride didn't marry him, she would marry no one, which must mean he was jilted at the altar and probably it happened here since he's murdering them in Vegas, but he and his ex-bride must have come from Mississippi."

"I hate to say it since it may be a bit of work, but can the records of local marriages be checked to see who applied for a wedding license and those who didn't file the thing back to the clerk's office, especially people from Mississippi?" I asked.

Lynn said it was possible to do that. It might take a while, but it was possible. She called Warren back in and explained the plot. He said it would be like a needle in a haystack to search through tons of applications. Lynn said everything was on computers at the clerk's office so that might speed the process. Warren asked if he needed a warrant. Lynn said it wouldn't hurt, so she called the DA and got his warrant. She said he could take extra men to help. He said that would speed up the process and left.

I thought about another way to go and suggested to Lynn, "You may need to contact wedding planners again and ask them to check their records for uncompleted weddings for brides from Mississippi. That may be a bit speedier."

Lynn grinned and said she would give that detail to Williams, that he needed something to occupy his time. She called him and told him what she wanted and hung up. "That will keep him out of our hair for a while."

"OK, this is a daunting task for the killer to find all the brides coming from Mississippi and get them lined up in alphabetical order, then stalk them for the kill. I'm not sure if I believe the angle of the home state, but it is a bit odd." Lynn pronounced the illogic of it all.

"Maybe the killer's bride ran off, and he's hunting her this way. He's not sure where she is, but he's tracking her down in this order. OK, I don't even believe that," I admitted. "He knows her, probably knows where she is but he can't bring himself around to kill her personally, just through surrogates of her. Why the alphabetizing? Was she a teacher, and made him do his alphabet each night before bed?" I grinned, thinking out loud.

"Whatever, I think we need to check on this Francis Langley from Mississippi who is getting married today," Lynn said as she stood. She took the list of brides and got Francis' information, then we headed out the back door to avoid going by Weber's office. I offered my SUV since it had lots of room to stretch out, especially for Deacon. He grinned at that and said that he missed all the razzing we used to give him. Lynn said to go to the Excalibur Hotel where Francis was staying. We arrived and went up to the suite that was given on the list. Lynn knocked on the door and it was opened by a rather elderly woman, around her seventies, who looked surprised to see four people and a dog.

117

"Hello, what can I do for you?" she said pleasantly, with a smile that reminded me of a kindly grandmother.

"May we speak to Francis Langley?" Lynn asked.

"Yes, I'm Francis Langley. May I help you?" she replied. We all were a bit surprised.

"Well, Francis, I'm Detective Lieutenant Lynn Carter, this is Detective DeAngelo and the couple behind us are civilian advisers.

"Is the puppy a police officer too?" the woman asked with a smile when she saw Willy in his bag that Penny had over her shoulder.

"Yes, he's a young tracking dog," I kidded. Lynn gave me an evil glance as I suppressed a laugh.

"May we talk to you please?" Lynn asked.

"Most certainly, young lady. Please come in, all of you." She opened the door wide and we went into the room. She took an instant liking to Willy and Penny, asking them to stand by her so she could pet Willy. She asked about the dog, then she stared at Penny and asked if she had a TV talk show. Penny said she did, and the woman was thrilled to meet a celebrity.

Bob Moats

It was a nice room. I had never been in the Excalibur Hotel, but I liked the layout of the room. I walked to the window, and there was a nice view of the MGM Grand and the New York, New York Hotel across the boulevard. The woman saw me admiring the view and came over quickly to the window. She pointed out the Tropicana on the other corner saying she stayed there years ago, back when this town was still run by the mob. She winked at me and said she had connections with the big boys. I was a bit taken aback, but said that was really interesting. She turned to Lynn, walked briskly to her, spry for an older woman, and asked what we needed.

"We have a strong lead that your life could be in danger. Are you from Mississippi?"

The woman looked surprised and responded, "Well, I have lived there for the last forty or so years, but my family and I came from New Jersey originally. When the Feds started to persecute my family, we all split up around the country. My parents moved to Mississippi. Frankly I hated it, too country for me. My family was linked to organized crime, but the Feds never could prove it, plus they wanted the big guys, not us underlings. Who's putting my life in danger, the Gigante or the DeCavalcante family? They didn't like my father. He threatened them too many times, God rest his soul."

Bridezilla Murders

Lynn was standing wide-eyed, at a loss for something to say. Deacon finally spoke. "Francis, may I call you Francis?"

She said, most certainly.

"We are on a hunt for a man who is murdering brides from Mississippi who are planning to get married here in Vegas. He's a serial killer, and we believe he may attempt a hit on you." Deacon figured she might understand better if he used the vernacular of the crime families.

Francis laughed and said, "I'd like to see him get to me. I have a whole pack of mobsters and hit men coming to my wedding. There will be more hardware there than the army owns."

Lynn said she didn't want to know. She asked if Francis would mind if she put a few undercover officers among her guests.

"Honey, you can, but I don't guarantee how the family may take the idea of police being that close to them." She laughed and said she would warn everyone, thanks for the concern. She escorted us to the door. As soon as she opened it, there were two huge no-necked men standing just outside. Francis said, "Ricky, it's all right, they're friends." The two gorillas moved aside and we went out.

We went to the elevators, and I said that was refreshing. I'd never been that close to a mafia princess. Penny said at her age she should be the queen.

Lynn said we had about five hours till the wedding. I said Francis didn't seem like a Bridezilla. Lynn grinned and said a mobster's daughter is more than a Bridezilla; they snap their fingers and have others break bones for them. She smiled, and we went down to the lobby of the Excalibur where we were stopped by three men in dark suits. They identified themselves as FBI and asked rudely what our interest was with the Mangelo family. Lynn looked confused and the lead Feebie rudely said the woman, Francis Langley is daughter to Carlo Mangelo, former mob capo from New Jersey.

Lynn flashed her badge and said to talk nice or she'd have his butt in a cell for being a jerk. The man smiled and then apologized; he said he just wanted to know about our interest in Francis.

"You mean you don't have her suite bugged? We're here on a hunt for a serial killer. We believe Francis may be an intended victim. That a good enough explanation for you?"

"Between our agents, the Mangelo family army, and your cops, the serial killer will be lucky to get anywhere near her." The agent laughed and they turned on their heels and walked off.

I said this was getting weirder and I hoped the Feds didn't interfere in our attempts to grab the killer. Lynn said either the killer was stupid or he would pass on Francis. This might be a bust.

Chapter 17

Back at Metro PD Lynn briefed the five undercover officers who would be covering the Langley wedding, warning them that there might be a little resistance from the guests. She explained the mob connection as the officers stood wide-eyed, silently worrying about being taken out to the desert by a couple of goons.

Lynn said that she and Deacon would be outside the chapel watching the building for uninvited guests. She arranged a place to meet at the chapel and turned the men loose.

Lynn turned to us and said, "You two may attend the wedding but it will be from outside. I don't want you to get in the middle of a gun battle if the Bridezilla killer decides to show. I hope we won't have another car chase, so I already have set up four cars around the perimeter of the chapel should he try to run. I'm also hoping he's still following his pattern and we have the right wedding. I'd hate to hear that some woman at another chapel was murdered while we watched this one."

We were at the chapel by 6 P.M. The wedding was scheduled for 7:00, but we had to coordinate the attack of our plan. Lynn had four men inside the chapel and one in the back rooms. Four cars were parked around the corners of the block awaiting orders if the killer headed off in a car. Penny and I stood off to the side of the chapel as Lynn and Deacon wandered around the outside of the building. I had a small Handicam that Lonie's cameraman gave me to document the wedding of a mob princess. Lonie was excited about that. I looked like a wedding guest taking videos of the whole thing. Lynn wasn't happy about her being taped, but I reminded her this would pay for our trip and she would be famous across the country as the officer who brought down the Bridezilla killer. She sort of liked that idea.

The wedding hour rolled around, and Penny and I stood at the chapel doors, able to see the proceedings as I was taping everything. Lynn and Deacon still kept a watchful eye on the building. Everything went smoothly, and I said to Penny that none of the guests looked a day under 60 years old. I wondered where the young mob wise guys were. Penny tapped me on the shoulder and pointed to the street where about six very tough looking men were waiting around the limo. The wedding ended, and they came down the aisle. Francis' new husband looked like he was about 105 years old, but he was spry enough to walk all the way down the aisle.

No killer popped up to fire at or attack Francis from the church as the bride and groom headed to a 1920s style Cadillac limo, fitting for the mob connection. I was getting some great videos. They drove off, followed carefully by the waiting patrol cars. Lynn and Deacon came up, and she said nothing, probably hoping for a sign or something to get the killer. We all went off to our cars and then over to the reception being held in a small banquet room in the Tropicana Hotel-Casino. It was fitting for the older gangsters in the group. The Tropicana still had the flavor and the interior of the '20s style Casino and Hotel. Francis chose well.

The reception was going well, plenty of toasts, jokes and stories of days gone by and tributes to the late Carlo Mangelo, the former Godfather of all in attendance. I was still videotaping, waiting for some Fed to come up and confiscate my tape. Strangely, some big gorilla was following Penny and me around. He had to be mob connected, maybe sent by Francis. I felt like I had a bodyguard. He smiled every time I looked at him.

I noticed a waiter give Francis a note. She read it and then got up, kissed her new husband and went through the kitchen door. I saw Lynn follow her shortly after, and then they both disappeared into the kitchen. I stood for a bit waiting for them to come out but they didn't. I went around to the door, looked in the small window and saw no one in the kitchen. That was odd. I looked at the gorilla and motioned for him to follow, telling Penny to wait out in the big room. The gorilla and I went into the kitchen. It was strangely silent. I motioned to him to go right as I went left, drawing my Glock from its holster. I heard a banging, went to what looked like a meat locker and opened the door. Lynn and five kitchen employees came rushing out, Lynn cursing and demanding my cell phone, which I handed her. She called Deacon and said to get every man into the kitchen now!

Cops came flying through the kitchen doors, followed by mob strong arms, then waiters who turned out to be Feds, everyone brandishing guns. It was a circus in the small room as Lynn filled in the men as to what happened.

The kitchen help told Lynn in the freezer that it seemed Francis got a note to come to the kitchen so they could ask her about the dinners, and then when she walked into the room, the killer grabbed her from behind and locked all the kitchen help in the walk-in freezer. Lynn came in and surprised the killer who still had hold of Francis. Lynn said the killer was wearing a George Bush mask and demanded that Lynn surrender her gun and cell. He told Lynn to drop both in a sink of water then took Francis out the back door after putting Lynn in the freezer also.

Bridezilla Murders

Lynn retrieved her gun and cell phone, shaking water out of both, as she yelled to get out the door and find them. The mob went out first, then our cops, followed by the Feds.

Penny peeked in just in time to see everyone heading out the back door. I saw her, took her hand and we went out after them. I was still videotaping everything. This was addictive; I might like being a news reporter.

There were about twelve men in the parking lot looking around for the killer. I figured since Francis was a bit past her prime she would slow down the killer a bit. My gorilla was still shadowing me. He was really into his orders. I asked him where was the limo, and he pointed to a part of the lot just off the boulevard. I saw the ancient limo sitting quietly by the road and then the lights went on and it started up. I yelled to Lynn and pointed to the limo. I heard her say, "Shit, another car chase."

The mob enforcers were fast. They got up towards the limo and started blasting the tires causing the limo to limp ahead. It stopped and the driver jumped out and ran across Las Vegas Boulevard, narrowly missing being hit by the speeding traffic.

The cops ran out, trying to avoid the traffic as the killer got across the street and into the Excalibur Hotel property, jumping barriers to get through the entrance. Visitors were amazed to see a man in a Bush mask being chased by about a dozen armed men as the killer disappeared into the crowd. The cops found the Bush mask and figured all the killer had to do was remove it and walk with the flow of tourists.

I got some really fantastic video of the whole thing and slipped the camera into my pocket so no one would want to take it away. Penny was bouncing up and down, excited by all the action and gun play. I told her to calm down or she would have to go to her room with no more excitement. She made a face and whacked my arm.

My gorilla smiled and said, "You want I should rough her up?"

Penny looked at him and then whacked his arm. He pretended like it hurt and grinned at both of us. I asked his name. He said it was Angelo. I said that if he ever moved to Michigan, I'd give him a job at my detective agency, and I gave him a card. He looked at it and asked if I had a good health plan. I laughed and said that was negotiable.

Francis was helped out of the wounded limo by her men. She smiled at Lynn as she went to her and thanked her for her quick actions. She said if Lynn ever wanted to join her family to let her know. Lynn blushed and said it would be an honor but she liked working as a cop. Francis went back to her reception being watched more carefully now by her men.

Lynn looked across the road to the Excalibur and said, "Well, the fucker did it again. He got away. I may lose my job if this keeps up."

Deacon was huffing as he came back across the road, dodging the fast moving cars. "We looked everywhere from the front to the back, but without knowing what he looks like, it was useless to try to find him in the crowd."

"Well, he's done for the night, I'm sure. We foiled two of his attacks. I'm sure he will be pissed, but he won't try anything more tonight. Francis will have a pleasant wedding night, if the groom doesn't drop dead from old age." Everyone laughed including my gorilla.

Chapter 18

Lynn said she would make her report in the morning, that she had enough for tonight. I looked to the gentle giant that was our bodyguard and thanked him, saying he did well and if we were ever in need of protection again, I'd call him. He just stood with no expression and we departed the place. Lynn, Deacon, Penny and I all went to our suite at the Bellagio and called room service. After a while there was a knock at the door. It was room service, but the man looked a bit apprehensive. I looked around the door into the hall and there was Angelo, my gorilla, standing there. He said he checked the cart and it was safe, no bombs or listening devices. I suppressed a laugh and said for the waiter to bring in the cart with our drinks and snacks. I grabbed Angelo's arm, pulled him in, and told him to sit and relax. Our lives weren't at stake right now so he could just be comfortable.

I asked him how he knew where we were. He said, "I got sources in the hotel and baggage handlers union. They know everything what goes on in the hotel. They told me your room number." That kind of scared me, but Angelo was so much like a big teddy bear, I let it go.

A half-hour later Buck and Maria showed up. Maria had finished her show for the night and they came to relax. My gorilla got up and looked like he was going to frisk them both. I told him they were friends. He smiled and shook their hands as I introduced them. Buck was eyeing the big guy who was about a head taller than Buck and about a hundred pounds heavier, all muscle.

We all sat and I related the events of the day to Buck and Maria. Buck said they explored the big

Outlet Mall north of the city, spending most of the day there, then went to get Maria ready for her show at the Tropicana. I said we probably missed each other at the Trop between the wedding and the show. I said we had a better show in the parking lot, if you liked gunfire and escaping criminals.

Lynn made a little grunt, apparently thinking about the killer still running around the streets of Vegas. She took out her cell phone and checked to see if it was still working from its swim in the kitchen sink. She was surprised that it did work, and she dialed William's number. He answered and Lynn asked if he got the wedding planners' lists of Mississippi brides who never made it to the altar. He said he had a stack of about 163 files from the last year that fit the bill. Lynn said to get the files to her in the morning and hung up.

"One hundred and sixty-three brides from Mississippi that didn't finish getting married. Can we just find one that turned her groom into our killer?" she moaned.

Everyone was relaxing, talking about different things, and I went to Angelo and sat next to him. I asked why he was following us around, and he said that Francis had told him to stick close to the dog lady from TV and her husband, to keep us safe. I smiled at the dog lady reference and told Angelo to thank Francis for us. He said he would. I told him he could go off to wherever he was staying or go explore Vegas, that I didn't think with two cops and my business partner here, he would be needed now. He smiled and thanked me, then got up, said good-bye to all and left.

Penny came over and said that it was exciting to have a mob enforcer as a bodyguard. I laughed and said our lives were so interesting. She agreed. I joked about Angelo's reference to her as the dog lady. She said it was better than a cat lady. I was imagining Penny at 80 years old having 40 cats all pooping around the house and me lying on the kitchen floor, dead and eaten by the cats. That would make Deacon happy. I'd have to tell him that.

I asked Lynn why the Feds were watching Francis, and she said the head agent told her that they watch crime families whenever they come to Las Vegas in groups. I asked if they were afraid that they'd try to move back and take over Vegas again. Lynn laughed and said that it was now a new crime syndicate running Vegas, huge corporations that ran the town, a completely different kind of mobster, the legal kind.

Buck said he wanted to go with us tomorrow to see what trouble we would get into. Maria had errands to run most the day along with yoga classes so she'd be busy. I said that would be nice since we hadn't seen much of him since we got there. He said he was having a good time and with only three more days to go he wanted to spread himself around. I said it would be good to have him on the case, we needed all the help we could get. I was thinking about the whole trip being paid for and was anxious to catch the killer.

Lynn started yawning and Deacon took the cue, saying they should go get some rest for tomorrow. They got up and left, then Buck and Maria took their leave and went off. I looked at Penny and asked, "Was it something I said?"

Penny laughed and said they must be getting tired of hanging around us old married people. She looked at me and asked if I wanted to go play the gangster and his moll in the bedroom. I said "Git youse butt in da bedroom, baby."

Willy spent another night on the couch. He didn't even move this time.

Tuesday morning was different; it was pouring rain. Vegas doesn't get rain often, but when it comes, it comes hard. The low-lying streets will flood and wash cars down the road if one is not careful. They have flood drains but when it really hits, even they can't keep up. I remember when I used to live there, coming around the back of the Imperial Palace Hotel and watching the river of water flowing out of the parking garage, flooding the street down to the concrete drain ditches that hopefully would take the water away.

Penny and I went to the hotel's parking structure, and I carefully drove the big SUV out onto the strip and over to Tropicana Avenue. We arrived safely at Metro PD and found Buck resting in Maria's car. I honked and he saw us, opened the car door and ran to the entrance of Metro PD as Maria waved and drove off. We all piled into Lynn's office after the desk sergeant waved us through. Lynn was going over the pile of papers that Williams had left for her of the Mississippi brides lists. Lynn stood taking the pile and dividing it equally amongst us, handing us each a pile.

"OK, read each one carefully. We're looking for a bride who stopped her wedding and left her groom stranded. If you can believe it, these brides are all from Mississippi. I hope that's a connection," Lynn instructed.

After a short while of looking, Buck cleared his throat and said, "Does the groom threatening his bride with death qualify him as a suspect?"

Lynn reached for the sheet of paper and read the paragraph that Buck was pointing to. It was a notation by the wedding planner about the outcome of the event. She wrote that the bride and groom fought all the way to the altar, then the bride told the groom to piss off and stormed out. Before she was out of earshot, the groom screamed that if she walked out, he would kill her.

Lynn looked up and said, "That's a valid cause for suspicion." She put the paper aside and kept looking through her papers. I had about two people that seemed suspect by the time I reached the end of my pile.

Penny came up with one that said the bride had called the police twice after the groom stalked her and made death threats. Police couldn't do much about it, so the bride left and went back to Mississippi. Didn't say what happened to the groom.

Lynn reached out, took the paper from Penny, and looked at it. Lynn said, "Seems the most violent of the lot. I'll call dispatch and have them look up the records of the day in question. This happened only last month. Maybe he's still in town." She read more of the paper, looked to me, and said, "Jim, this says the bride's occupation was a teacher. Maybe she did have him do his alphabet each night before bed." She smiled.

I asked what her name was, she looked up and grinned. "Her name was Zora. Last letter of the alphabet."

Chapter 19

"I guess he wants to go through the entire alphabet before he gets to her. But he'd have to go back to Mississippi to do that unless he lures her back here," I offered.

Lynn got on her phone, called dispatch, and asked if they could pull up all the information on a couple of 911 calls. She gave them the date and the name of the caller. She hung up and looked at the file again.

"The groom's name is Harry Norton. There's no other info here in the wedding planner's file other than he lives in Jackson, Mississippi." Lynn went to her computer and typed the name and keyword Mississippi into the LEIN system. Nothing came up relating to him. She got on the phone, called information, asked for his name, city and state, and was told that there was no phone number listed for that person. I said to try Google. She gave me a dirty look and then decided to try it. Surprisingly, there was a website connected to his name that was listed as "I_hate_Bridezillas.com." Lynn clicked on the link.

Bridezilla Murders

I came around to the computer, looking over Lynn's shoulder, reading the heading of the page. There wasn't much there, just a picture of a moderately attractive woman with a big red X through her face and a short paragraph about how this woman tore his heart out by rejecting him at the altar. It continued saying that his bride was a Bridezilla and he now wanted all Bridezillas to pay for the humiliation that they put their men through. He had been subjected to the worst treatment that any man shouldn't have to go through. He would become the champion of the downtrodden and shamed men who had their hearts torn from their bodies. His mission was to destroy the Bridezillas, cleansing the earth for better marital bliss.

Lynn said that we had a confession and our killer.

Lynn called Williams back in and told him to check around the hotels and motels within fifty miles and see if he came up with a Harry Norton. He grimaced and went out, grumbling something we couldn't hear.

I asked Lynn if I could use her computer for a moment and she got up. I went to the Whois website and typed in I_Hate_Bridzillas.com address and then hit enter. After a couple of seconds, the details of the website's owner came up. It had Harry Norton's name as administrator and technical contact. The address was listed as a P.O. box in Vegas. I looked at the DNS server name, wrote down the address listed, and did a Whois search on the name. The details came up as a webhost company in Las Vegas. I showed Lynn and said that if she could call them, they might be able to tell her his address locally. He would have to pay them for the website somehow, and it probably would be attached to an address.

Lynn called the webhost company but was rather rudely told that they didn't give out clients' information over the phone. Lynn called the DA and asked for a search warrant, then told us she was going to that place and would shove the warrant right up that bitch's ass. I wanted to laugh but Lynn was in too pissed of a mood.

I said it was strange that Harry would go to the trouble of putting up a website and then spend time killing these women from Mississippi and doing it alphabetically. It also meant he had a computer or laptop with connection to the Internet. Maybe he used the public library or an Internet café with Wi-Fi. I was thinking about the classmate killer using the Pompo Deli Internet to send out his threatening emails.

Lynn's phone rang, and she had her search warrant. We packed up and slipped out the back to avoid Weber. Lynn and Deacon went in her unmarked cop car and Penny, Buck and I in my SUV. Willy had his head hanging out of his bag looking half asleep. I reached over and roughed up his head. He shook it out, giving me a dirty look. At least what I thought a dirty look from a dog was like.

Bridezilla Murders

We arrived at the Digital Highway webhosting company and went into the building and up to the reception desk. Lynn came up and asked the young lady seated at the desk if she was the person who answered the phone for her call about Harry Norton. The girl looked at Lynn's gold police badge clipped on her blazer and said nervously that she was. Lynn waved the warrant in her face and said she wanted to talk to someone in accounting. The girl got on the phone and made the call. About two minutes later a man came out and asked if he could help us. Lynn showed him the search warrant, explained what she needed, and the man told us to follow him.

Lynn pushed me out front since I was the computer nerd of the group, and I explained that we were hunting down a serial killer that might have started a website on their servers. He looked surprised and asked what the domain name was. I told him. He punched a bunch of keys on his computer and looked a bit distressed at what he saw. I asked him under the search warrant if he would bring up the man's details of his account with the webhost. The accounting tech who introduced himself as Al Martin brought up the detailed statement of Harry Norton's account with Digital highway. It was brief, having just started this month, and amazingly had no address other than a P.O. box. The account was paid for by money order. Clever killer.

Lynn sighed and said she'd have to fight the federal government with a search warrant for the P.O. box info. She said they didn't give out P.O. boxes without some kind of identification as to residence and citizenship to prove the person wasn't a terrorist. I asked Al if I could access Harry Norton's internal files on his site. Al stood up after hitting a few keys and said to go to it. I sat and brought up the directory listing of all the files on his site, the ones that people couldn't see unless Harry wanted them to see. I explored and found a few files that looked interesting. I pulled out my flash drive that I always carried, plugged it into the USB port on Al's computer, downloaded the files to it, then turned the controls back to Al. I asked Al for a printout of all the relevant info regarding Harry's account on their servers. He obliged. I gave the printout to Lynn. She thanked Al, and we took our leave. As we left, Lynn gave the receptionist a big smile. She said she wanted to give her the finger, but decided against it.

We went back to Lynn's office where I plugged the flashdrive into Lynn's computer and opened up the files. I laughed and said, this guy's not stupid, he's putting his personal files on his web space rather than leave them lying around on his computer. I showed Lynn the first file. It was a list of all the women who were reported by wedding planners as being Bridezillas, listed by state, then by wedding date, then named alphabetically by first name.

Bridezilla Murders

"He's just taking them as they come off the list. I guess he's not fussy about them being alphabetized, just keeping them in order. He's probably OCD. The state of Mississippi is listed first, most likely since his Bridezilla came from there. He's placed an X in front of the completed killings. The ones that we fouled up for him are listed with a question mark."

Lynn asked if Norton would know that we had this list. I said no, he'd never know we were in his website directory. She asked who was next on the list. I read down all the names until I got to the Gs. "There are two Gs from Mississippi. The first listed, Gabrielle Westfield, is getting married today at 3 P.M. Then there's a Gloria Davis also marrying today at 7 P.M. He's got a backup on this one," I explained.

Lynn looked at the clock on the wall and said we'd have to move fast, there were only four hours to go to protect Gabrielle.

~~*~~

Across town just off the I-95 freeway, a billboard was having a new sign pasted up on its surface. It was a huge picture of Captain Weber with showgirls surrounding him, photo manipulated, most likely. To the right of the picture were the words, "Las Vegas' Most Popular Comedian! Watch for him!"

Score five for the Vegas Jokers.

Chapter 20

Lynn assembled another team of undercover officers to get inside the wedding, then she checked the map on her wall to coordinate the unmarked cars outside the wedding chapel. This was not going to be an easy feat. The chapel was right on the strip, one of those small quickie type places to get hitched, like where Brittany Spears celebrated her nuptials to her hometown boyfriend. This would also be a challenge for the killer. It was crowded at the chapel with all the tourists milling about.

I suggested he might take a quick shot at her with a gun and get lost in the crowd. Lynn snarled that maybe we should give the bride a Kevlar vest. I remembered the one I wore when I was shot at by Ralph at the courthouse.

Lynn told her undercover men that if nothing happened at the 3 P.M. wedding they had to get over to Viva Vegas Chapel for the second wedding. This was going to be an interesting day.

About fifteen minutes later, while still plotting our plan, we could hear Captain Weber screaming from his office, yelling that he wanted an arrest warrant out on Trapper for anything they could nail him with. Deacon went out and talked to one of the officers up front and came back to relate the latest gag Trapper and Becker whipped up. He said a patrol car was cruising the freeway, saw the billboard and called it in to see if Weber had decided to go into show business. Deacon said Weber was having fits.

Lynn announced that we should all vacate the building before Weber took his wrath out on us. We slipped out the back door and drove over to the Venetian Hotel to track down Gabrielle Westfield. Lynn got the same reaction from the desk clerk as she did at the Hilton, but they gave her the room number. We found the room, knocked, Gabrielle answered the door, and, after identifying ourselves, Lynn explained our intentions of watching her wedding to protect her from a killer. Gabrielle scowled about having to put up with extra guests at the small wedding and looked a bit angry. Lynn assured her that the officers would stay in the background and not interfere with the wedding. She swore and said she didn't like cops being around her wedding.

"Gabrielle, we have three women in the morgue and one in a coma at Desert Springs Hospital. I don't want any more murders in my city. We will watch you whether you like it or not, or I'll take you into protective custody and you'll have your wedding in a jail cell. Like it or not we will be there." Lynn snarled, not liking the prospect of Vegas becoming a great place to die on your wedding day.

142

Gabrielle opened her mouth to speak, but stopped, shut her mouth and went into her bedroom. She came out with her wedding dress and said she had to get ready, could we all leave. We left her to her ritual of preparing for her nuptials and went to the chapel to check the layout of the building and the activity on the street out front.

"This is going to be tricky for the killer," Lynn proclaimed.

"And grabbing an elderly bride in the middle of mob wise guys, cops and Feds wasn't tricky." I laughed.

She acknowledged, "OK, OK, I'll admit this guy is gutsy or real stupid. We stopped him twice, and we will stop him again. There won't be any more bride murders in Vegas..."

"As long as we keep stopping him," I finished.

She gave me the same dirty look I was getting used to by now. She turned and went into the chapel to scope out the rooms off the main wedding chapel.

"I called a couple of men to go and follow Gabrielle over here, but I think she'll be safe till the wedding starts. Lately our killer likes to wait up to the ceremony, either just before or after," Lynn observed.

"You yourself said he was escalating, each time a different weapon, getting worse in how he handles the brides. He changes modes, his attacks. He's like more than one person in one body. This man is psychotic, a serial killer even without the Bridezilla connection, but he found his MO, his meaning in life, murder neatly wrapped up in an excuse for vengeance. He was hurt by a woman who rejected him at the altar of his love, but is there something deeper?" I said, then shut up.

Lynn looked at me and asked, "What brought on the psych 101 evaluation?" I said I didn't know, maybe I was channeling Mickey Spillane. Penny looked at me and said I was just weird.

The bridal entourage arrived and went into the chapel, followed by the cops, all trying to look inconspicuous. Penny and I watched from the chapel doors again as I taped everything on the small camcorder. The wedding was quick and was presided over by another Elvis preacher. Penny expressed her displeasure at the imposter, and the happy couple ran out of the chapel in a hail of rice from friends and relatives allowed to attend. Penny said there was no justice in the world. Penny knew that birds would attack the rice thinking it was food, and the rice would either stick in the bird's craw or expand to cause problems for the birds. I loved her compassion for lesser creatures.

Gabrielle and her new mate went to the waiting limo to take them to the reception at their hotel. The undercover officers followed closely. Lynn, Deacon, Buck, Penny and I hung back and stood watching them go.

"My men will watch her during the reception and notify me if there is trouble. We now have another wedding to attend to." Lynn sighed, took us to our cars and we drove to the New York, New York Hotel then went up to Gloria Davis' room after checking with the desk clerk. We went through the same warnings and arrangements with Gloria that we did for Gabrielle, and all ended up at the church where Gloria's wedding took place. The men were planted in amongst the guests and stationed around the grounds, but this wedding went off with no problems either. After the happy couple left we just stood around wondering.

"OK, we have no attacks. Is the killer catching on to us, or are we at the wrong weddings?" Lynn lamented.

I thought about all the prior attacks, and then I had an idea. "Lynn, the first Bridezilla was killed trying on her dress; the second was killed after she finished her arrangements; the third was attacked with a pipe at the church after calling off the wedding, but the kill was foiled. So he tried again at the next wedding, and after she called it off, he kidnapped her and murdered her in the basement. Next came Edith, and she successfully got married, so the killer grabs her and the groom, but he is stopped again. Now he waits till Francis is married and grabs her at the reception. OK, foiled again. But now we have two weddings that make it to the receptions and no problems. What if the next step is the wedding night, nuptial bliss in the privacy of their rooms? Do you see where I'm at?"

Lynn stared at me for a bit then the lights went on. She got on her cell, called the troops in, and had them go to the women's hotels and interrupt them. She said that Gabrielle was next on the list so we would go there.

About twenty minutes later, speeding through the streets with flashers and sirens, we rolled up to the Venetian Hotel, roaring up to valet parking and jumping out of our cars. Deacon yelled at the parking attendants to leave the cars alone. We piled into the elevators and went up to Gabrielle's room. Deacon got there first and banged on the door, calling out to open up. Buck, Penny and I held back from the area, letting Lynn and her cops take charge of the situation. Gabrielle opened the door and screamed, "What is the problem?" The cops all piled into the room and did a search of the entire place, closets and all. Nothing came up. Gabrielle was pissed. Lynn apologized and came out yelling that we had the wrong place. She put two cops on the door and told them to stay alert, then we headed back down to the lobby and out to our cars. We all drove over to New

York, New York Hotel and up to Gloria's room. Lynn found the door open, and she and Deacon went in carefully with guns drawn. I held my gang back again as a precaution. The living room was empty, but in the bedroom they found the groom unconscious on the floor.

Lynn was in agony now and called for all units and available men to get to the New York, New York and help to search for the killer.

Chapter 21

"Crap, we don't even know if he's still in the hotel. He could be long gone by now." Lynn was pacing the floor, waiting for back-up. She sent some of the men that came with her out to scour the hotel and called EMT for the groom who was just coming around from a blow to the head. She called Hotel security, told them of our situation, and asked for help.

I had a thought and went off to the hall, followed by Penny and Buck. I called the Excaliber Hotel and asked to be connected to Francis Langley's room. I waited and she came on.

"Hello, is this the new Mrs. Traviano?" I asked politely. She said it was. I continued, "Ma'am, this is Jim Richards, the dog lady's husband. Remember me?"

"Of course. How are your wife and that cute little pooch?" She was pleasant.

"They're fine. I'm calling with a small problem. We have another bride abducted and I was wondering if Angelo was nearby that I could talk to him."

"Oh, dear, I hope the bride will be all right. Yes, Angelo is in the next room. I'll get him for you." She evidently carried the phone out in the hall as I could hear a door opening and closing, then a knock. I heard voices and then Angelo came on.

"Mr. Richards, good to her from ya," he said happily into the phone.

"Angelo, I need your help. Remember when you found our room that night in my hotel, you said that your sources in the union knew what was going on in the building?"

"Yeah, I got friends on the inside who have an ear to the goings on. Where ya at?"

"We're in the New York, New York Hotel. I need to talk to someone here who can help us with another bride abduction in the hotel. Someone who knows what's going on in the place."

"That would be Jimmy Knuckles. Sorry, his name is Jimmy Karpis. He's union steward in the place. I'll have him call you."

"Please be quick. Every minute counts, and thanks, Angelo, I owe you one."

He hung up, and I just stood looking at my wife and Buck. Lynn was on her cell phone pacing between the room and the hall. Finally, after five minutes, my cell rang. I answered, said hello.

A rather gravelly voiced man asked if I was Mr. Richards. I said I was, and he said Angelo told him to fully cooperate with me in anything I needed. Good old Angelo.

"OK, here's the story. I'm helping Vegas police, and we just had an abduction in your hotel. We're up on the fifth floor, and the person taken was a bride." He said he heard about the bride murders from the news. "Yes, this is the same man. I need to know if there is anything you could tell me, ask your employees here if they saw anything suspicious in the last hour."

He said he'd get on it and call me back. I grabbed Lynn on her pace out of the room and related the story of Angelo and his union buddies. I said I was waiting for a call from him after he inquired of the staff. They had to have seen something. They were all over the place. Lynn's face turned a little happier than it had been and she thanked me, asking me to keep her informed. Just then my cell rang and I answered. It was Jimmy Karpis. I put the call on speakerphone so Lynn could hear.

"Mr. Richards, cleaning service says a cleaning cart and laundry hamper was taken from service room six on the fifth floor about two hours ago, and they don't know where it went to. The tenth floor people say a man with a cleaning cart came out of the elevator, went down the hall to a room and went in. They thought it was strange, but one of the girls said it might be an emergency clean up. Sometimes people get a little too drunk and mess the bathroom, if ya know what I mean. They said they didn't recognize the man, but our turnover rate is high so he could have been a new man."

"Are your people still on the tenth floor?" I asked.

"Yeah, they're prepping a couple rooms for new guests. I'll call them and get a fix on the room." I said thanks and hung up. Lynn yelled to her men in the area and called for everyone to get to the tenth floor. We all piled into the elevator and went up five floors slowly. I asked Lynn where was hotel security. She said they were watching all the entrances and exits for anyone trying to take the bride out.

We got to the tenth floor and found two maids in the hall. Lynn asked them if they were the ones who saw the cleaning cart. They said they were, and Lynn asked them which room the man went into. They pointed down the hall and gave the room number. Lynn asked for their pass card, and the one woman said she'd open the door but couldn't surrender her card or she'd get fired. Lynn said that was fine, but to get out of the way as soon as she opened the door. The maid said not to worry, she'd move fast.

The maid opened the door, and all the cops piled into the room. I kept my gang outside. Lynn and Deacon stormed around the room and heard a noise in the bathroom. They carefully came to the door. Lynn peeked in the door crack and saw a man doing something in the room. They burst into the room with guns up and calling for the man to freeze. The man looked stunned and held his hands up, saying, don't shoot, he was just cleaning the toilet. Lynn looked over and saw the mess that someone had left in the toilet, clogging it up. The man had towels around the base of the toilet.

My cell phone rang. It was Karpis again. He said that he just found out the room we were in was scheduled to be cleaned due to a mess made by a guest. But there was a laundry basket in the hallway of the back delivery bays that shouldn't have been there. A van was seen parked in the bay as the workers came in. It was being blocked by a semi dropping off supplies for the hotel. I called to Lynn and told her. She looked to one of the maids and said to lead them to this service bay, now. She yelled to me to have Karpis block the van, hold it till they got there, but don't do anything else. I gave Karpis the message. He said he'd have another truck block the bay up good.

We followed the troops down to the first floor, through the back halls of the hotel and out to the delivery bays. The van was still sitting there with three trucks blocking its exit. Lynn, Deacon and the cops stormed the van and found the bride in the back under a pile of bed sheets, unconscious, but the killer was gone. Lynn said he probably slipped out the delivery door, realizing he wasn't going anywhere with the van.

I looked around the bay, saw the ever present surveillance camera and pointed it out to Lynn. She barked some orders to her men to take care of the bride then went to the hotel security man standing at the bay door and asked to see the video of the bay. He led us to the operations center where banks of monitors had an eye on everything going on in the casino and hotel.

The head security person had one of the tech men show Lynn whatever she needed. She started with the video of the hallway of Gloria's room. The tech went back two hours and ran fast forward till they saw a man in a hotel uniform pushing a laundry cart to the room. He did something to the door and it opened.

Security said he might have gotten hold of a master door card. He went in. Lynn said she wished they had cameras in the rooms, but that was not permitted.

Nothing going on, so the video was fast-forwarded again to when the bride and groom came to the door. It looked like they were arguing as they went in. About a half hour later the killer came out with the cart and went down the hall. Lynn complained that the man kept his head down. His face was hidden by the baseball cap he was wearing all the time he was in the hallway. The tech did his best to follow the man through the hotel with the cameras in each area until he reached the delivery bays. He pushed the cart to the van and opened the side door. He looked around, still hiding his face under the cap, grabbed an arm full of bed sheets along with the bride and dumped it all in the van. He looked around again and got in the driver's seat, started the van and attempted to drive forward just as the semi pulled across the door. The killer sat there waiting, we could see him, then he looked back, saw something, jumped out and ran through the outer door. Just then Lynn and Deacon appeared, missing the killer by seconds. Lynn swore and sat back.

Chapter 22

Medical techs were working on the bride and groom. They were both conscious and trying to answer Lynn's questions. She was getting no more from them than she already knew. They had no answers. Detective Warren came up to Lynn and pulled her aside.

"I knew that your inquiry on Norton's info came up a bust so I did a bit more digging and finally got hold of his fiancé. He lived in Mississippi for less than a year, hadn't applied for a driver's license there, and he lived with his fiancé, so filed no address. Based on her info I did some more digging and came up with this." He handed Lynn a manila envelope that contained a blow-up of a driver's license from Virginia for Harry Norton.

Lynn exclaimed that she could kiss Warren, but Deacon warned she better not. Warren just smiled and went off. Lynn held out the photo for all to see. She now had the killer's picture. She looked at it and said that Edith's description for the sketch artist was actually very close.

I said the TV news was covering the bride murders, why not plaster this picture all over the TV and shake this guy up, maybe even find him faster? Someone might see him. Lynn did a few seconds of meditation, then said she had to talk to someone and went off leaving Deacon and us to wonder.

We saw her on her cell and then she gave the picture back to Warren. They talked a bit, then he went off in a hurry. Lynn came back to us and said she had the wheels of justice in motion. She explained that by tomorrow morning the picture would be all over town, in newspapers, on TV, and copies of the picture would be sent to every casino and hotel for security to watch for him. She had arranged for officers to watch the airports, both McCarran and North Vegas airport in case he tried to skip town now that they had his image to go on. She talked to the police commissioner and said he was making a formal statement for the media and would give a press conference in the morning. Norton's ass was toast.

A rather burly man came up and asked who Jim Richards was. I said I was. He introduced himself as Jimmy Karpis. He said he was sorry that we missed the killer and wished his info had been more accurate about the first sighting that sent us on a wild goose chase. I said that he at least told us about the delivery bay van and that had saved the woman's life. Lynn said to tell his network of employees that the LVMPD appreciated their efforts to help. He smiled and said he would, then went off.

Bridezilla Murders

I looked at my watch. It was almost 10 P.M., and I realized we hadn't eaten since this morning. I said I was treating if everyone wanted to go to the Subway by the MGM Grand. Lynn said that she and Deacon had to go file their reports or they'd catch hell. So I said we'd see them in the morning and took Buck, Penny and Willy off to get something to eat.

We departed the New York, New York Hotel and I was driving over Tropicana Avenue to go to the Subway just across the Boulevard when I saw it. I started laughing out loud, and Buck asked what was the matter. I pointed to the taxi in front of us, and Penny and Buck joined my laughing. On cabs in Vegas they have what they call taxi tops. These are the small signs on the car that are used to advertise shows and events around town. You can't miss the things, and the taxi in front of us had a taxi top with the picture of Captain Weber standing in front of the Vegas background with big lettering across the bottom, "Weber for Mayor, he's your man!"

Score six for the Vegas Jokers.

My cell phone rang. It was Deacon asking if we had seen any cabs lately. I said I was looking at one right now. Deacon said he got a call from Tim Carney. It seems Weber got a call from the Mayor asking about his candidacy, and Weber was flabbergasted. Trapper was getting into deep shit. Now he'd involved the mayor.

I relayed the info to my gang, then we parked and went to Subway and ate a good meal. I tried calling Trapper on his cell, but all I got was voice mail so I left a message saying he'd better lay real low, and hung up. I said that I hoped Trapper wasn't going to run out of money. Billboards and taxi tops aren't cheap. I know because when I was working for Nicky North here in Vegas, I had to pay all the bills for his show. Billboards and taxi tops could get expensive.

Buck's cell phone rang. It was Maria saying her show was over and she wanted to know where Buck was. I told him to invite her to our room and we'd get room service. She said she'd see us shortly and hung up. We went back to the Bellagio and up to our room where we found Maria already there. I called for refreshments, and we settled in for the night until they left around 1 A.M. Penny and I played Gangster and the Moll again. Willy just ignored us old people and slept on the couch.

Wednesday morning was beautiful, bright sun and blue skies. We had a good breakfast sent to our room and ate in bed, a little treat we deserved. About a half hour later there was a knock on the door. It was our cops. Lynn asked if we had breakfast yet, and I said we enjoyed it in bed. She went to the bedroom where Penny was still lounging and snatched up a piece of bacon from her tray. Penny yelled an obscenity, one I hadn't heard her utter before, and had Lynn laughing.

157

Bridezilla Murders

"The commissioner will be on TV today at 9 A.M. and hopefully we will have a spotting of our killer. There were a whole lot of blow-ups sent out and emailed to the media," Lynn said between bites of bacon. She was sitting on the bed with Penny saying how nice the mattress felt. Penny made faces at Deacon and me and asked us to leave the room. Deacon made a strange little noise. I said to come with me and I'd tell him about the strip club I took Penny to and the hot female dancer who hit on Penny. Penny yelled to go easy on that story.

Penny and I dressed while we were all were watching the news broadcast of the commissioner as he proudly held up the photo of the Bridezilla murderer as he called him. I said I hoped Francis didn't take offense to being referred to as a Bridezilla or the commissioner might end up in the desert. Lynn said that she had this case on high priority, and every available man was working it. The commissioner then said that the efforts of the entire LVMPD were working night and day to bring the criminal to justice. I looked at Lynn and said, she just said that. I also said maybe the commissioner should run for mayor instead of Weber. Deacon laughed and said Weber was still smoking about that; he pitied Trapper if Weber got hold of him.

I asked who the next victim would be if the killer went on without concern for the visual exposure. Lynn said it was a Holly Franklin, getting married today at 5 P.M., and she had an idea that might work if they received no response from the photo release. She told us her plan. We all thought it was good, but Deacon had his reservations about it. Lynn told him to get a grip and help in her plan. I thought the plan was good, but it might be dangerous if not done properly. Deacon agreed. Penny called us both wusses and said it would work, she could feel it.

Buck called and said that he and Maria were going down to visit Boulder City and might even go visit the Boulder Dam. I said not to jump off the thing or get pushed and hung up. I looked at Deacon and said that Maria was really taking Buck's time here. He grinned, saying he hoped that he didn't end up with a brother-in-law. Although Buck was a pretty cool dude, he joked.

I said Buck was the farthest person from getting married, but I agreed that Maria could be persuasive. I also wondered what devilment Trapper and Becker were into today and hoped they would keep their heads down. Deacon said he knew Trapper to be a worthy adversary and would chew his leg off if caught in a trap. We all laughed. Penny gathered up Willy and we went out of the room.

Chapter 23

Lynn and Deacon were ahead of us in her unmarked car. I could see them from our vantage point and saw Lynn answering her cell phone. She finished the call, and my cell rang. I figured it was Lynn. It was.

"Jim, got a puzzle. I just got a call from Warren. Seems we have another bride murdered. She's in an apartment off Maryland and Flamingo. Fiancé called it in. Follow me." She hung up.

I wondered why the killer was changing his pattern. The next wedding wasn't until later today unless he was pissed by the press conference this morning and went after a random bride. That just didn't settle. Why put a careful plan together only to deviate from it? Was he that upset that he had been unmasked and wanted to confuse the cops with a diversion?

I told Penny what Lynn said and tried to follow her in the crazy morning traffic on Flamingo Avenue. We arrived at an apartment complex near where I used to live just off Flamingo Avenue. We pulled into the apartment complex. I could see the cop cars parked by one building along with the meat wagon. Penny and I were asked to stay out of the apartment till Lynn could get an idea of what was involved. I stood at the door with my now ever present mini-cam in hand, sighting in on the scene that I could see.

A woman was lying on the floor in the middle of the living room, blood pooling up around her, a wedding dress crumpled on the other side of her. Lynn was talking to a man who looked very distressed. The mini-cam had a directional microphone on it so I plugged in the earphones I had and could hear the basic conversation. Lynn asked the man to sit down and wait for her. She came out the door followed by Deacon.

Speaking to no one in particular, she said, "OK, this guy says he came here to this apartment where his fiancé was staying with a girlfriend and found her dead on the floor. He called the police and is claiming it's the bride killer. The woman's name is Vera West, and she's from Baton Rouge, Louisiana. Doesn't fit our killer, now does it?"

"Either a copycat or the groom is lying. I'm betting on the groom," Deacon offered. I quietly agreed.

"Where's the girlfriend?" Penny asked.

"The man says she wasn't here, she was at work. Warren is trying to track her down for a statement. This sounds bad to me. The Bridezilla killer could now become an excuse for angry grooms to whack their brides. We have to catch this guy before he becomes a hero to beleaguered grooms everywhere."

161

Lynn went back in the room and told the former groom to follow her. Lynn called for a uniformed cop to take him to the station and settle him in an empty interrogation room. The cop left with the man. Lynn consulted with the ME and the head CSI, and we went on to Metro PD.

Coming down the hallway from the back door, Weber breezed by us without even a word. That worried me. He looked really distracted, but was smiling. That worried me even more.

Lynn directed Deacon, Penny and me to the observation room as she went into the room on the other side of the mirror. Penny let Willy out of his bag to walk around the room, giving him some exercise, she told me. Deacon said he loved to watch Lynn question suspects, that she could get them to confess to just about anything she wanted.

I knew there was an art to interrogation. Many good cops could bring out the good or bad in a suspect. I had seen enough of it in my first year of being a P.I. and being allowed by my new police friends to observe questioning, both here and back in Michigan. I knew it wasn't proper procedure for me, a civilian, to be allowed in on the investigation, but I always tried to help and usually did. It was also nice to be trusted by the police.

Lynn sat down across from the groom and asked if he was read his rights, just as a formality. He said yes. She asked if he minded having the questions video recorded. He asked if he was a suspect. Lynn explained that she had to question everyone who came in contact with the crime scene and that, until proven otherwise, everyone could be a suspect. The groom argued that it had to be the bride killer; it was on the news every day. Lynn asked again if she could record the conversation. The man agreed.

"OK, state your name."

"Michael Gregory," he replied curtly.

"How long have you known the deceased, Vera West?"

"About three years. We met through work."

"And where is work?"

"Baton Rouge Realty. I was a salesman, she was a secretary. She was so lovely and smart," he replied staring at the mirror.

I always felt uncomfortable when people stared at the mirror, like they could see me sitting there watching them.

"Did she have a temper?" Lynn asked.

He turned his eyes to Lynn and said, "She could be mean, yes. But we loved each other so you just overlook the bad things about a relationship."

"Bad enough to murder for?"

"What are you implying? I said this was probably the bride killer, didn't I?"

"You called the police about an hour before I arrived. The ME said the bride had been dead about two hours. You just missed the killer, didn't you?"

"I guess you could say that," he replied.

He was squirming now, looking uncomfortable.

"Mr. Gregory, do you know what an MO is?" Lynn shot at him.

He stared at her and said no.

"It's short for 'modus operandi.' It means an unvarying or habitual method or procedure, basically that a serial killer will do his murders consistently the same, with a plan." She sat back and let that sink into West's brain. She leaned forward, almost resting her head on her arms that lay on the table and looking him squarely in the eyes. "The Bridezilla Murderer has a formula for his murders. That way we kind of have an idea of what he is going to do next. The murder of your fiancé wasn't in the plan that our killer had. She wasn't murdered by our killer. Have any idea who may have wanted Vera murdered?"

He was quiet and then said he wanted a lawyer.

"A lawyer, Mr. Gregory? That implies that you may have committed the act. Now, we can get you a lawyer and you can go to trial and have a jury sentence you to life or worse, or you can confess and save everyone a lot of time and trouble. Maybe even get you a lesser charge if you killed her in a rage or were frightened for your life. You decide."

Lynn got up, said to think on it, and left him alone in the room. We sat watching his face as he mulled over the possibilities. Lynn came in with us and called him a weasel. I said, don't be too hard on weasels. Lynn smiled, and then West yelled that he wanted to talk. Lynn went back to the room and had a pad and pencil with her this time.

"OK, what do you want to do, Mike?" she asked trying to soften him up for the kill.

"I want to state that she made me do it. She pushed me way too far this time." He made a face that showed anger and yet a satisfaction in his crime.

"You're saying that you killed her in an angered rage? She was goading you to do it by being mean to you?"

Bridezilla Murders

"Yes, she was harping on the wedding and how I wasn't doing enough. Shit, I tried to help, but she kept yelling at me that I was doing everything wrong. Fucking bitch!" He wept, and went quiet. Lynn waited for him to speak again. "I saw the knife on the counter. She was screaming like a mad woman, then she started shoving me and hitting me. I hated her. I just couldn't take her anymore. She was not the woman I fell in love with. I grabbed the knife as she came at me and held it in front as she rushed into it. I didn't even try to stab her, I just held it in front of me and she ran into it. Honestly!" He wept harder.

Lynn pushed the pad and pencil in front of the man and said when he was able to, write down everything that happened as he just told it. He put his head on his arms and sobbed. Lynn left him alone.

I had a choke in my throat and both Deacon and Penny were silent. Deacon finally broke the silence. "It never gets easier."

Lynn came in after a bit and said they had no more to do here, that she had called the DA and they would take it from here. We had matters that were more pressing. The Bridezilla killer was still out there.

Chapter 24

Lynn said we had to get our minds back into the Bridezilla killer now that we had been sidetracked. Lynn said in order for her plan to work she needed Shelby Francis' help and called her. She explained what she was going to need, and Shelby said she'd be happy to help out. Lynn and Penny went out leaving Deacon and me on our own. Deacon said that we could go over to the church where the wedding was going to be and scout it out. We got into my SUV and drove up to St. Michael's Church, walked around the property, then went in to meet with the priest who was to perform the wedding and explained what was possibly going to happen. The priest looked upset, but we assured him that there would be plenty of police around to see that everyone was safe.

Lynn called Deacon to tell him she was ready and they'd meet us at the Rio Hotel where the bride and groom had their room. We drove over, met our women at the entrance to the hotel, and went in. Lynn already had the room number and we went up. Lynn introduced us to the woman, Holly Franklin, and asked if we could speak to her. She invited us in and asked us to sit.

Bridezilla Murders

"Miss Franklin, we have a strong lead that you may be the next attempt by the bride killer you may have heard of."

The woman looked struck, said she had seen the news about the murders and asked why she was included in the victims. Lynn gave a quick rundown on the killer's MO, and Holly just sat listening.

After Lynn finished, Holly stood, went to her purse, took out a badge and showed it to Lynn. She was a homicide detective for the Biloxi, Mississippi, police. Lynn laughed and said she didn't know. Holly said that her fiancé was a police captain for vice, and they came to Vegas to get away from crime in their city.

Lynn looked at Deacon and said that maybe she didn't need to execute her plan. Holly asked what that plan was, and Lynn told her she was going to switch with the bride just after the ceremony, go out for the limo ride to the hotel and hopefully catch the killer. Holly smiled and said she had done her share of undercover work and had nabbed a number of bad guys so she was more than happy to help catch the killer.

Just then the door opened and this very big man, almost bigger than Deacon, came in. He was surprised to see a bunch of people and one small dog in the room. Holly introduced everyone to her fiancé, Mark Gladman, and told him about the threat on her life. He took it all in and asked what would Lynn like them to do to help catch the fucker. We sat making a new plan and settled everything just up to the time to get ready for the wedding. Holly said she never thought she would have to be armed under her wedding dress and laughed.

Around 3:30 we all headed to the church, and Holly went into the bride's room to get ready. Mark asked Deacon if he'd like to be included in with his groom's men, seeing there were only two survivors of his police friends that came with them. Deacon smiled and said he didn't have a tux. Mark laughed, tossed one to him and said it was one that a third friend was supposed to wear but he got sick that morning, too damn much partying last night. Mark said Deacon and his friend were about the same size, and Deacon went to a room off the groom's room to change.

Penny and I were allowed to sit out with the guests, and we sat on the bride's side. I had my mini-cam going and was glad Lonie gave me a pocket full of tapes. I saw Lynn with a camera, probably police issue. She was going to pretend she was a wedding photographer during the wedding in case the killer tried anything then. We discussed the fact that since the killer had gone through the entire wedding process from starting at the planner's to the honeymoon suite, we weren't sure at what point he would come in now. So we just wanted to cover all bases.

Bridezilla Murders

Lynn was all over the place taking pictures and getting the eye from the real wedding photographer hired by Holly's wedding planner. Lynn had informed Shelby that the plan had changed and thanked her for the loan of an old wedding dress that Lynn borrowed for the original plan, promising to return it.

Lynn was surprised by the inclusion of Deacon in the wedding party and had to laugh at the sight of him in a tux. Lynn came over to us and said she might still put on Shelby's wedding dress and get Deacon to marry her later.

The wedding started, and Holly came down the aisle as both Lynn and the photographer snapped shots of her. The ceremony went smoothly. They proceeded out to the front of the church, and Penny was delighted to see they threw birdseed.

Into the limo they went after Lynn came around and snapped a couple pictures of the driver. She had cars stationed around the area in case, but she felt that there would be no problems.

Penny and I went to the Rio Hotel where the reception was to take place, followed by Lynn and Deacon in her car. I called Angelo again and asked if he could put me in touch with the union steward in the Rio; he said he would be more than happy to and hung up. A little later my cell rang, and I talked to the steward and explained what we would need from his employees. He said that he would put out the word for anything suspicious.

The reception was going well. This was the third one we had attended, including our own. I was beginning to feel like a wedding crasher, and the food was getting better. Willy loved the bits of food Penny gave him as we sat at a table with about six young kids. We ended up there since the arrangements didn't include us originally. The children were getting a kick out of Willy, like they had never seen such a small dog before.

It was about 9 P.M. when the bride and groom announced they were retiring for the night and thanked everyone. Lynn followed them, still taking pictures, up to the elevator. Holly and Mark thanked Lynn for watching them and said they would see her upstairs. Lynn and Deacon went to the next elevator and got on. Lynn punched the button for the sixth floor that the bride and groom were on and up it went. They arrived and got out, finding they were alone on the floor. Lynn looked at the elevator lights and saw that it was on the floor below, probably for someone getting on.

Penny and I had stayed on the ground floor and were watching the reception from the hall by the elevators when my cell phone rang. Lynn asked where we were and I told her. She asked me to watch the elevator that the newlyweds got on, it was heading back down. It stopped on our floor and the doors slid open. The thing was empty.

I called Lynn and told her. I heard the word, shit, and she hung up. I called the steward again and told him that we had a possible abduction on the fifth floor. If he had anyone on that floor could they check to see if they saw a bride and groom along with a third person and let me know? About three minutes later my cell rang. It was the steward saying that room service had seen them going to the stairs at the north end of the hallway. I asked him to keep track and let me know. I called Lynn to let her know. She thanked me and hung up.

Upstairs, Lynn had called hotel security, filled them in on the events, and asked if they had an eye on newlyweds around the fifth floor and heading down the stairwell. The section head said that they were watching them going down the stairwell and that they had reached the ground floor which leads to the casino. Lynn warned them this was the Bridezilla Killer and to just watch them and keep her informed, that she had her men on it.

Lynn and Deacon were already on the way down the same stairwell and moving as fast as gravity would take them. I got another call from the steward saying they were spotted in the casino by the front of the building on Tropicana. Penny and I were just around the corner from there, and we rushed around to see Holly and Mark looking like they were being herded to the front doors by a man in a baseball cap. I told Penny to hold back as I rushed over with my hand on my Glock and stepped in front of them at the doors to the street.

I acted like I was drunk. "Excuse me but I was here first I think. Do you mind waiting for me to get my bearings while I try to get out of here, friend?"

Mark looked down and saw that I held my Glock to him, shielding it from the sight of the killer who was yelling at me to get out of the way. Mark took the Glock, and I raised my hands to the guy and said pardon the hell out of me, then stepped back as they went out. I followed. I figured Mark wouldn't want to use the gun in the casino, too many people, but out on the street the playing field was narrowed.

I stood just behind them as Mark stopped and said he was not going anywhere with the man. The killer pulled out the gun he had and pointed it at Holly, saying to move now, just as Mark brought up my Glock and fired point blank. The killer went down just as Lynn and Deacon came running out of the casino.

Lynn got on her cell and called for an EMT unit and for her men in the building, then she took the killer's gun from Mark who had taken it from the killer's hand as he squirmed on the pavement. A crowd was starting to gather, and the extra cops arrived to do crowd control. Lynn studied his face and recognized him as the one in the driver's license. She looked up at us and said we had our killer.

Chapter 25

Mark came up to me and Penny, handed my Glock back and said that was gutsy and crazy, but he thanked me. He said he had thought about carrying his weapon, but figured with all the cops around he didn't really need it. He also said that he was actually a good shooter, but didn't want the killer dead, so he just winged him.

Lynn came over after talking to Holly and getting her story. She smiled at me and said that I should apply for membership in the mob since this case had their help, and she thanked me for my actions in getting the weapon to Mark. She also said she might have to take my Glock to test for the shooting, but she'd wait till someone asked for it.

Lynn turned to Holly and Mark and laughed. "Why are you two still here? You have a wedding night to celebrate."

They took their leave and ran back into the hotel. Penny and I hugged on the sidewalk and Willy tried to squeeze up between us to lick our faces. I let him this time.

The EMTs had Harry Norton all trussed up on a gurney, and Lynn ordered Warren and two men to go along and keep an eye on him. She came back to us. With Deacon standing next to us, still in his tux, she kissed him. He blushed saying, stop that. Lynn said she never could resist a man in a tux. She whispered something in his ear. He blushed again and asked if she still had it. She nodded. I knew he was referring to the wedding gown and that someone would be play-acting a wedding night without the ceremony.

Penny asked if I had recorded the abduction attempt, and I said I left the thing on all the time up to where I was at the door. I even got Norton being shot. Should be good for an Emmy award. I said we had our story to give to Lonie to give to Gordy for his special on the crime of the century featuring the brave heroine Penny Wickens-Richards, and the trip would be paid for. That made me happy. We went back to our SUV parked in the Rio parking, drove out Tropicana, went one last time up the strip to look at the lights, and then turned at Fremont Street and back down to the Bellagio.

When we arrived back at our hotel, Lynn and Deacon said they would show up later for our last night in Vegas. Lonie came by after we called and told her we had great footage of the capture of the Bridezilla Murderer. I gave her the camera and tapes and said, don't lose them. She laughed and said, not on your life. She was thrilled and said she'd get this to Michigan when they went back tomorrow and that she'd see us at the airport.

I really hated to think our trip and wedding was over. Crap, a whole week and we hardly got to relax and celebrate. Penny kissed me and said she'd make up for it later. It was just after 10 P.M. and we crashed on the couch. I looked at the couch and said, "Doesn't matter where, here or at home, we always end up on the couch."

Penny's cell phone rang. It was Gordy. She answered and he said he talked to Lonie who was excited by the footage that they and Jim got of the crime. He was bubbling, almost sickening to hear. He said to get him the final bills for the whole week and submit it to accounting, that they'd take care of it. He said he'd see us later and hung up.

I was ecstatic that the whole thing would be paid for and kissed Penny, thanking her for the whole week.

"What did I have to do with it?" she asked.

"Well, you called Gordy to get the plane out for everyone by arranging for our wedding to be recorded, then when we got here the crime came up and the crew started to record everything, which led to Gordy agreeing to paying for everything. This is your doing. So thank you."

"Well, you better remember that. You now owe me a big one." She smiled and kissed me. I resisted a crude remark about a big one and kissed her back.

Lynn and Deacon, followed by Buck and Maria, came in around 11:00 carrying a huge bottle of champagne. I had to call for room service for extra refreshments and extra glasses. The staples arrived, and we celebrated Penny's and my wedding and the capture of the killer.

Later Buck came up to me as I stood by the window looking out at the sights of the city I loved. "Jimmy, I know you'd be hurt if I wasn't around to help you fight crime, although I didn't help much this last week. Maria is to blame. She and I have been talking, and we may consider getting together some time soon." He was hem-hawing around. I pretty much figured what he wanted to say. "I really like Maria, and she looks great in feathers." He snickered. "I really think I could get along with her, and we talked about it."

"Crap, I bring Deacon out here and he stays. Now you're saying you may be staying, too. I have to stop bringing friends out here. Everyone is staying but me." I laughed.

Bridezilla Murders

"I haven't decided yet. It's in the talking stages. Maria says she can get me a job at some big bike shop out here where she knows the owner. It's a full blooded Harley shop, man. Damn, that would be nice."

"Buck, if you want to live with Maria or get married, you have my blessing. I'd miss you, but I want you to be happy." I put my arm around his shoulder and gave him a noogie. He struggled out and gave me his walrus smile.

"Hell, I'm not one for domestic life, you know that. I'm going back to Michigan, but I'll probably be coming out here more often to stay with Maria for a couple months then back to home. My family and friends are all back there. I'd hate to leave that. But I want to see if it would work. Maria is some woman." He went back to Maria, and I just stared out the window at the fountain out front. It was no longer pink, and I wondered what Trapper and Becker were up to. I'd find out tomorrow when they would go back with us to Michigan. I hoped they were having a good time on their last night in Vegas.

I watched out the window at the lights of Vegas shining and flowing and the traffic on Las Vegas Boulevard streaming north and south, all the tourists and locals going to destinations unknown, and wondered if I could leave my family again and move back here. Penny had no family back in Michigan. That was sad. My family had adopted her and she might have a problem leaving them, too. I did it once before and thought I could do it again. I didn't want to be cruel to my family but I had my life to live, too. Well, it now included Penny, so it was our life now.

Penny came up to me from behind and whispered in my ear, "Penny for your thoughts."

I laughed and said that was an offer I couldn't refuse. I told her about what Buck had said.

"Do you think you would ever want to move back here to Vegas?" she asked while holding on to me from behind, her head resting on my shoulder.

I paraphrased a line from a book I once read about Vegas. "Once you've lived in Vegas and got sand in your shoes, you can leave, but you'll always come back."

She hugged me tighter.

"I'm drawn to this place. Yes I could, but it's a big change for everyone. You, me, my family. I have the money that I could bring my family out here to visit often but..." I paused.

"But what?" she asked.

"I don't know. Would you be happy here?" I asked.

"Are you kidding? I've grown to love this town. All the lights, the excitement, the murders—well, not so much that. I could easily live here. But then I don't have real family anywhere to hold me down. Your family is now mine, but I'm not hooked on them enough to make myself stay in Michigan. My place is with you now. We are husband and wife, and I honor that. I live where you are and I hope you give me the same respect and love." She came around to my front, put her arms around me, and kissed me full on the lips.

Deacon was making kissy noises, and then everyone started to make kissy noises. I just yelled for everyone to grow up. I told them to get the hell out, it was late and we were tired and had to fly back to Michi-boring-gan tomorrow. Deacon said we just wanted to have sex, and I threw a pillow at him from the couch. Everyone laughed, said their good nights and went out. I looked at Willy who was lying on the couch looking at us. I said, sorry pal, but you know the drill. Penny and I went to the bedroom and closed the door. Willy huffed and put his head back down to sleep.

Chapter 26

We were up early finishing the packing we started last night. Everything was back in its place, and I knew I didn't have to do it, but I left a tip on the night stand for the cleaning people. I had a new appreciation for them after the help we received tracking down the killer.

Penny, Willy and I went down to the lobby and settled our bill, making sure I had a copy for Gordy. I looked at it and was very glad I wasn't paying for it.

We drove the SUV over to the MGM Grand where I returned it to the car rental place and got another copy of the bill. Deacon was meeting us out front to take us to the airport, and we found him and Lynn sitting out front in a police cruiser. I said it was nice they brought the limo. He laughed and said Weber wanted a police escort out of town for us to be sure we left and that we took Trapper with us.

I felt weird in the back of the cop car, and Penny said it was the first time she had been detained by the police.

When we arrived at McCarran Airport business terminal, our plane was waiting. I saw Buck and Maria but didn't see Trapper and Becker; I wondered if they took a commercial flight back. We took the baggage out of the car and set it by the baggage Buck had on the ground. Lonie and her crew unloaded the van of their equipment and set it by our stuff. Lonie smiled, and I said that Gordy called us last night, very excited. She said they had gone over the video I shot and it was really good. She asked if I wanted a job on their news team. I said I'd think about it.

Maria was talking to Buck and then gave him a big kiss. She said to us that she had to leave for a rehearsal for a new routine in her show then left.

A few minutes later a cab came driving around the hanger and out popped Trapper and Becker, both smiling widely.

"Good to see you're still free men. Weber's been looking for you," I said as they came up and put their bags by ours.

"Well, that was one hell of a week. I took Barry to see my old home, and we did a lot of exploring the town, other than a few diversions we cooked up." Trapper was still grinning widely.

"I suppose you ran out of money with the billboard and taxi tops?" I asked.

"Hell, no. I know the right people and have a few dark secrets about people in the company that services the advertising. I got it rock bottom, just for the paper and printing." He laughed.

"Well, you made an impression on Weber," Lynn offered.

"I've never seen him so red as when he found out about the billboard," Deacon added.

"Barry, I hope you didn't learn any bad habits from this man?" I asked Becker.

He grinned and said, "Trapper warned me never to pull anything like this back home. I'll be booking drunks for the next year if I do."

We were about ready to put the baggage in the cargo hold when a big black Escalade with black tinted windows roared around the building with blinding flashers. It zipped up to within a couple yards of the baggage and out jumped three dark suited men in sunglasses, the kind Feds took to wearing. They approached us. Two went around the back of Trapper and the other came up to him real close.

"William Trapper, I have a federal warrant for your arrest. We are officers of Homeland Security, and we are arresting you on charges of conspiring to subvert the government by sending covert messages from various points in Las Vegas to factions in the terrorist community. You will surrender, or you will be arrested by force under section 12 point 2 of the Homeland Security Act of 2002, and transported to a federal detention holding facility in Los Angeles." The man was speaking calmly and coolly.

We all were shocked, and I could see Trapper was stunned. The two officers handcuffed Trapper as he was yelling that he did nothing subversive. He yelled to Deacon to get him a lawyer and find out where they were taking him. Deacon had a strange smile on his face, and I was wondering about that. The Homeland Security agents took Trapper towards the SUV just as a back door opened and out stepped Captain Weber. He was laughing and yelled, "Gottcha!"

Trapper's jaw just about fell to the ground, and he yelled, "You old son of a bitch!"

Weber came to Trapper, gave him a big hug, and said it was good to see him again. He told the "agents" to remove the cuffs and they did.

I looked at Deacon. "You knew about this, didn't you?"

"No, I was as surprised as you until I recognized one of the agents as Steve Rawlings. He works in vice over in south Metro PD precinct. I then knew something was going on."

Weber gave Trapper a hard stare and said it was real good to have him back in town and getting his blood pressure up. "Now, I want to actually see you get on that jet and go back to annoying your Captain in Michigan. Oh, and I called him to fill him in on your escapades here. He enjoys a good joke, too."

Trapper was really speechless now and quietly said, "I'll miss you, Captain."

Weber quietly said, "I'll miss you, too."

Weber yelled to the three "agents" to help get the baggage on the plane so they could get this scumbag out of town just as Lynn's cell phone rang. She listened and had a stunned look on her face. We all stopped to wait for her to finish.

She went to Weber. "Captain, Harry Norton, our bride killer, somehow overcame an officer, took his weapon and shot him. He's critical but alive. Norton took Detective Warren hostage and left the hospital. He got away with Warren in tow by hijacking a car in the parking lot. There is an APB out, but they disappeared before any squad cars could get a fix on them. They're gone."

Weber was stunned and told his men to get back in the car and go to Metro. He yelled to Lynn to get on it now, and then they were gone.

I couldn't believe what I heard. Warren was a decent guy and I had come to like him. I just couldn't go back home now, knowing his life was in danger. I looked at Trapper and said, "shall we help out?" He said Warren was a friend, and he never deserted a friend.

I looked at Penny and she said, "let's find the bastard and get Warren back." I asked Deacon if we could hitch a ride back to town. He said he'd be more than happy to. I gave our apologies to the pilot and asked if they could hold over a day or two. He smiled and said he'd love to visit Vegas. Lonie was stunned to find the crime still worthy of news, told her crew to put the equipment back in the van and offered to take any baggage we had that wouldn't fit in the squad car.

Lynn, Deacon, and the rest of the gang piled baggage into the van and got ourselves into the police cruiser. Buck and Becker went in the van, and we all drove over to the Tropicana after I said I'd like to stay there and it was on the way to Metro PD. Deacon dropped us off and said they had to go to the precinct and get more info. I said we'd be in touch. We all went into the Trop, and I registered everyone in rooms, including the camera crew. What the hell, Gordy would be paying. Lonie had called Gordy and filled him in on the facts. Gordy said to go for it and bring back great footage.

Bob Moats

We dropped off our baggage in our rooms and went down to the car rental in the Trop. I got another SUV. I was beginning to like the damn things. We all drove over to Metro PD, followed by the news van. Trapper and I went in leaving everyone else outside. Too many people to attack the fort, I said. Lonie came over and slipped the mini-cam and a couple extra tapes in my pocket, saying, just in case. I asked Buck to man the SUV in case he needed to move fast. He climbed into the driver's seat and said he had it covered.

The place was on high alert; all available officers were out on the road looking for the car, now identified as a 2009 brown Mercury Marquis. No plates were spotted but it was different enough to stand out.

Lynn was in her office with Deacon; she was on the phone with the third officer at the hospital getting filled in on what happened. Trapper and I stood at the door of the room while we waited for Lynn to finish. Trapper had clipped his badge on the outside of his jacket; I couldn't do the same, so I just stayed close to Trapper.

Weber came barreling down the hallway and saw Trapper and me. He smiled and said it was good to have us men in to help find Warren and the killer, he appreciated it. He looked at Trapper's badge then looked at me and called to Lynn to deputize me. He stormed off. I was a bit surprised, but I had done enough work for LVMPD, I felt like one of the cops.

Lynn came to me and said to raise my right hand. "Do you swear to blah, blah, blah and uphold the blah, blah, so say you." I smiled and said I do. She handed me an auxiliary officer's badge and said, don't get shot.

Chapter 27

Lynn told us to come in and sit down, that nothing could be done until they had a sighting of the car.

"It seems that Norton faked an attack and was shaking violently in his bed. The officer in the room called for a nurse and went by the bed, something he shouldn't have done. Norton grabbed the officer's weapon and shot him. He jumped out of bed just before Warren entered into the room. Norton was behind the door and surprised Warren. He took him out of the hospital, hijacked a car in the parking lot, and made Warren drive. This is from various eyewitness accounts. They drove north on Maryland Avenue, the last time the car was seen.

We sat in silence for a short time waiting for the phone to ring with news. Williams poked his head in the door and said they had the County Sheriff, North Vegas Police and Henderson Police on alert also. Lynn thanked him, and he left.

I called Buck and asked how everyone was holding up outside. He said they were all relaxing as Becker filled them in on how they did all the pranks this last week. I said I'd keep in touch and hung up. I looked at Trapper and said Becker was spilling the beans on their villainy this last week.

"Barry is a good kid. I'm going to really try and get him ready for promotion. He deserves it," Trapper said.

The phone rang and Lynn listened for a minute then said they found the car out in a parking lot just off Charleston Boulevard and Maryland. There was a report of another hijacked car. The victim said there were two men and one had a gun on the other. "At least we know Warren is still alive."

I asked if they had an address on Norton since his arrest. She replied they couldn't get any fix on where he was holed up the last month he lived here, and he wasn't talking. I asked if Warren had a GPS on his cell. Lynn said they tried that, but the phone was found in the hospital parking lot in some bushes. Norton caught on to our last attempt to track him that way.

Bridezilla Murders

"I remember Greg Warren when we both started as rookies here on bike patrol. He was always cheerful and always had a joke for the day. I really hope he gets out of this safely." Trapper sounded worried.

I asked Lynn if she ever got a response from the Post Office about the P.O. box. She said it came up to a fake address taken off a fake ID card that the Post Office just took on faith. I asked if she had a copy of the fake ID. She opened the file and pulled it out then handed it to me. I asked if I could use it for a short time. She said feel free. I went out to the hallway followed by Trapper. He was curious. I called Angelo again. I now had his personal cell number that he gave me when we last spoke. He came on, and I said it was me.

"Mr. Richards, I'm glad ta hear from youz. Howz da wife?" he said in his best New Jersey accent.

"She's great. I need to ask you a question." Angleo said shoot, then laughed at the word shoot. "I know that your family doesn't involve itself in any illegal activities in Vegas, but I wondered if you may know someone in town who's a quick paper artist and may have whipped up a real good Nevada ID for a person that we are looking for."

Angelo was quiet for a second and asked if this was on the QT. I said I wouldn't bring any cops down on his contact, strictly informational. He was quiet again and said he'd call me back. I hung up, looked at Trapper, and said it was better than sitting around.

He smiled and said, "Now I know why I like you. You're sneaky."

About two minutes later, my cell rang. It was Angelo. He said that there was a guy he heard about that could whip up paper for any state for a sizable fee. I asked if I could see him. Angelo said that his contact told him it was all right to ask him questions, but it had to be over the phone. "He don't want no contact with the cops." I said I could do that, and he asked if he could give the guy my number. I said to do it, he said OK, then he hung up.

My cell rang a few minutes later and it came up on the caller ID as unknown. Cautious guy. I answered, putting it on speakerphone so Trapper could hear. The voice said he was doing a favor for Angelo and asked what I wanted. I said I had an ID that was a fake Nevada ID for the Bridezilla killer. I asked if he heard of him. The voice said he had, and if he made paper for the guy, he didn't know the guy was a scum bucket. I said if I showed him the ID, maybe he could tell us something about the guy so we could find him. He said to meet him at the Grocery Outlet on Maryland and Charleston. I said I knew the place and we'd be there in twenty minutes. He said he'd be wearing an I love Vegas hat, and hung up.

Bridezilla Murders

Trapper and I made excuses for leaving. We went out to my SUV, and Buck slid over so I could get behind the wheel. We drove over to the Grocery Outlet that my son and I used to shop at all the time when we lived here and parked away from the building. I got out and said that Trapper was to follow, but everyone else stay in the car. We went around and found the guy. He was nervous and eyed Trapper as a cop. I said he was OK, and we just wanted info. I said my name was Jim and this was Will, and the man said we could call him Lester. I showed him the copy of the ID the Post Office made of the killer's ID. He studied it a bit, then said, yeah, he made it for the guy. Lester asked if this was really the bride killer, and we told him it was. He said shit, and then said if he knew, he would have called the cops himself.

I asked if there was any little thing that the killer might have said or done that would point us to him. Lester said that the killer took him to his bank so he could withdraw the money to pay for the ID. He said that the guy was stupid, and he could see the account number and pin as he entered it. Lester said he had a photographic memory and took out a paper and wrote the numbers for us. He said it was a Wells Fargo bank on Rancho that they went to. I thanked Lester and slipped him a fifty. He thanked me and went off.

Trapper said, "Why the hell did you give him a fifty?"

"I like to keep people on my side. Haven't you ever paid an informant?"

"Well, yeah, but not a fifty. A twenty, yes, but not a fifty."

"This is Vegas. A fifty is chump change. But he took it, so I got him in my pocket now."

Trapper just shook his head and said I was sounding more like a mobster the more I did this.

We went back to the car and I called Lynn and explained what we just found out. She asked for the numbers and I relayed them to her. I said maybe the bank account had an address attached to it. She said it most likely would and hung up. I looked over to my team and said I was hungry, so we went over to Charleston to the nearest burger joint, bought take out and went back to Metro. I brought in the extra bagged burgers for Lynn and Deacon. They thanked me, then we all went out to the parking lot to eat with the rest of our crew. Lynn said she was waiting for a search warrant for the bank account and just sat on the curb looking at me, eating her burger.

"Do I have to worry about you and your mob connections now?" she asked between mouthfuls.

I grinned and said, "Hey, blame Penny. Francis took a liking to her, and we ended up with Angelo on our side."

Penny spoke up, said she was a TV star, and couldn't help it if she had a following, even in the family. Lynn laughed for the first time since Warren was taken. Her cell phone rang and she answered. She stood and said we had our search warrant then went to her car followed by Deacon. She yelled that one of the DA's people would meet us at the bank. We all drove over to Rancho Drive and into the bank's parking. We all piled into the bank and asked for the manager. A woman in her fifties and looking fit came up. Lynn showed her the warrant and asked for the account information on the numbers she had. The manager took her to a terminal, typed in the info and printed out the statement. Lynn looked at it and smiled. She came to us and said, "We have an address."

Chapter 28

Lynn got on her phone and called Weber, saying, "Thanks to Jim Richards and his mob connections—I'll explain later—we have an address for Norton. I can't say he's there but we are going over to check, and need back-up and a warrant." She gave him the address and said we'd wait for support to arrive.

We drove to within a block of the address and watched the house. I asked if she had a make on the second car Norton hijacked, and Lynn said it was a dark green Ford Focus. I said that I would cruise by and take a look. Lynn had the patrol car and said she'd wait. I drove the SUV past the house. Trapper glanced carefully at the house. I told everyone else to look forward as we drove by. I heard Trapper make a little noise that sounded like, yes, and we went around the block, back to Lynn and Deacon. I pulled up behind them and Trapper jumped out telling Lynn that the Focus was in the drive, back by the garage.

Lynn got a call on her car radio that back-up and SWAT were just around the corner, arriving in a couple of minutes, and they had the warrant. Lynn and Deacon went to the trunk, took out vests and told Trapper and me to hold back for our own safety. Trapper reached behind his jacket, pulled out his service piece, and said just try and stop him from coming. Lynn sighed, flipped him a vest and said it was his neck. Trapper looked at me and asked me to stay with the rest. He looked concerned. I said I would. Becker asked if he could come. Trapper looked at him and said his orders were to protect the civilians. Becker said he would. I think he was glad Trapper didn't let him go.

The three of them went down towards the building, staying close to the front of the houses that made up the quiet little street. I hoped there would be no shooting. Just as Lynn, Deacon and Trapper approached the house, all the back-up and SWAT vehicles roared up and everyone piled out. From where we were, I could see Deacon at the front door with about eight men covering his back. Lynn went around the side with the rest of the officers. Deacon banged and did the 'open up, it's the police' thing, and then he went through the door like it was balsa. The men all streamed in, and it got real quiet from our vantage point. I saw an officer run out, go to one car, and grab a med kit. He went back in the building. I looked at Becker and said to watch everyone, and I went to the house.

I made sure my junior cop badge was clipped to my jacket and then I carefully went in. I could hear various voices yelling, "Clear," and I heard Deacon yelling for an ambulance. I came around the corner from the living room to the hall and saw men standing by a door. I went up and looked over their shoulders and saw a woman lying on a bed, beaten up and bleeding as two of the officers administered first aid.

Lynn came up behind me and said, "You just don't listen, do you? That's the trouble with you mob guys."

"I take it Norton and Warren aren't here," I said.

"Just found her. She said she's the woman who owns the house and she let Norton stay here. She saw Norton bring Warren in. After seeing the news with his picture, she told him to get out. He beat her. She'll live, luckily, but Norton took Warren and went off in her car. She gave the description of the vehicle, and I called it in. This is not getting better. The only good thing, Warren is still alive." She frowned and started to walk away.

"And Norton has no address now. He may force Warren to go to his home. Does Warren live alone?" I asked.

Lynn stopped and stared at me and said, "Sometimes you amaze me. Warren lives with another cop. They share a house over in Red Rock Canyon. I'll call for the address and see if I can get hold of his housemate." Lynn yelled out loud that we all had a new place to go to and stormed out of the house followed by the pumped up officers. Trapper was on my heels as I ran back to the SUV, and we climbed in and followed the entourage of Lynn and Deacon in the lead car. They all had flashers and sirens blaring, and I tried to keep up without killing anyone. I wasn't exactly trained to do high speed chases. Trapper yelled, next time he drove.

We drove west on Lake Mead Boulevard and down to Warren's street. Lynn had reached Officer Dan Billingsley of North Vegas Police, Warren's housemate. He said that he'd meet us at the house since he was closer. Lynn warned him to wait for her team, and he agreed. We pulled up to the address and saw Billingsley by his car down the block; he knew the routine. Lynn had everyone kill the sirens about a mile from the house so as not to alert the killer if he was there.

Lynn didn't need a warrant since it was Billingsley's house and he gave us permission to enter. Everyone crept down the row of houses and came up to the ranch style home with desert landscaping. I thought Warren had good taste. I was at the back of the group with Trapper, and then all hell broke loose as the SWAT and the cops descended on the place. Billingsley opened the door with his key, and everyone piled in. I heard shots coming from the back of the house, and Trapper and I ducked behind a small shed on the side of the building. Trapper looked around the shed and ran to the back side of the house just as a man ran past him towards the front of the house. I was still watching from the shed and saw the man coming towards me. I grabbed a rake leaning against the shed and dropped it in front of the fleeing man. He tripped on it and went down just as a whole gaggle of cops came around the building. They swooped down hard on the fugitive and brought him up to face Lynn and Deacon as they ran up. She looked at the guy and said it wasn't Norton.

After the dust settled and the house was checked, Lynn managed to get a confession from the perp. He was in the wrong place at the wrong time, robbing the house. I had to suppress a laugh at the criminal's misfortune; it was actually funny. Poor guy was pilfering the place and had a dozen cops plus SWAT converge on him. I'm sure he crapped his pants.

"OK, Norton didn't bring Warren back here. So where did they go? He'd have to settle somewhere, and dragging an extra person around doesn't make it any easier." Lynn stomped around.

"I think Warren will be safe for a while. He's Norton's safe passage ticket. He'll use him to get by us," Deacon said.

Williams came up and said they had a team checking and informing motels in the area to be on the lookout for Norton. He didn't think Norton would risk using any of the big hotels with Warren in tow. He went off.

Norton could be anywhere in Vegas or out of Vegas for that matter, I thought. Penny, Buck and Becker were standing out on the front sidewalk talking. Penny had Willy on his leash that was stowed in the doggy bag so Willy could get exercise and do his doggy do-do. He looked so funny, such a tiny animal, bouncing around looking like he had no care in the world. Such a simple life.

Lynn's phone rang. The caller ID said it was a friend she had in the local media, a reporter for KLAS-TV. Lynn answered and said she had nothing for her, then went quiet and went to the TV that was in Warren's house. She turned it on and we all gathered around it.

The news bulletin was already on. "... and police have been in pursuit of the bride killer since his escape earlier today from the Desert Springs Hospital after seriously wounding one officer and taking a police detective hostage." The woman news anchor paused as she was handed a paper. "This just in, we had a call from the killer saying he has demands of the police if they want to see Detective Warren alive again. We are in communication with Las Vegas Metro PD and have gotten in touch with Captain Theo Weber with the demands of the bride killer. We will be following this breaking news story as we receive...." Lynn hit the off button just as her phone rang.

"Detective Lieutenant Carter," she said into her phone and listened. She hit the end button and yelled for everyone to pack up and go back to HQ. She looked at Trapper and me and said, "The killer is getting worried. He wants a helicopter to Mexico and a million in cash, or he says Warren is toast."

We all went back to Metro PD and into the big conference room that was usually used to hold big functions. This qualified. Weber, whose first name I now knew was Theo, stood at the podium and yelled for quiet. There were about thirty cops in the room and a number of office and support people, all of whom were friends with Warren.

Weber cleared his throat and said, "Norton called KLAS and gave his demands to them so he would have the attention of the citizens of Vegas. This, he figures, will make us yield to his demands. For the sake of Detective Warren we will do what we can to agree to his demands, but when we get Warren back, it's an open-season skeet shoot for this fucker. I didn't say that, but I'm sure everyone here understands."

The crowded room all made noises of support, then Weber called for Lynn and Deacon to meet him in his office. He called the meeting closed and stormed out.

Chapter 29

Trapper and I stood outside Weber's door as Lynn and Deacon sat listening to Weber relate the demands that Norton made to the media. "Norton wants one of the tourist helicopters from down on the strip and a million dollars in twenties, all by tonight or he will start, as he says, carving up Warren a piece at a time and sending the pieces to us by FedEx."

I could tell Norton was an idiot. If he wanted the demands fulfilled by tonight, then sending anything by FedEx would delay his plans. Also a million dollars in twenties would be a huge package, almost too big to put in the small helicopter he wanted. The guy was not in his right mind.

He was making a show of his advantage over us. We wanted Warren back, and he knew it. Weber's phone rang and he answered then went to his computer. He sat and typed in the address for Norton's website 'I_hate_bridezillas.com.' He did this because he was told Norton made a call to KLAS again and Norton said for them to go to his site. KLAS wasn't going to run the website on their news until they let the police see it. We gathered around the back of Weber, looking at the monitor as the first page came up. The picture of Norton's Bridezilla, Zora, was gone and now replaced by a picture of Warren tied up to a chair and gagged.

I said, "Norton must have taken along his laptop and was somewhere he could get on his website and update the page." I looked at the room that Norton had taken the picture of Warren in and made a funny noise, a happy and yet choking noise. Everyone looked at me, wondering if I was having an attack. I said I recognized that room. I said it was set up exactly like the mob lady Francis' room. I know because I liked the way it was laid out. Norton somehow got into the Excalibur Hotel!

The room went nuts. Weber and Lynn both got on phones and called for troops to gather to make a plan of attack. Lynn looked closely at the picture and said it was definitely the room set up and had the features of the room that she stood in while filling in Francis about the bride killer. They went to the war room, as they were calling it now, as officers gathered and Lynn filled them in on our new discovery.

Trapper followed me as I went off to the side. He figured I was up to something. I called Angelo again and asked if they were still in the Excalibur Hotel. He said they were, and I filled him in on what was happening. He said the TV news had cut into his viewing of "Jeopardy" so he knew about the abduction of our cop friend. I told him that the killer was in his hotel, and I would appreciate it if he could do his magic and find out anything of importance for me. He said he would and hung up after I gave him some facts and said not to let his people do anything other than surveillance.

Trapper smiled at me as we went back to Weber's office, but everyone was now heading out to go to the Excalibur. We ran to our SUV. Everyone was watching Buck's new tiny portable TV with the coverage of the abduction and the latest breaking news about the website.

I drove over to the Excalibur and, as we arrived, my cell phone rang. It was Angelo and he was excited. He had info that two men checked into a fifth floor room and they had very little baggage, just a laptop and one small suitcase. The bigger man was looking very distressed, and the smaller man had his hand and arm covered by a jacket. One bellman was going to carry the suitcase, but the small man yelled at him and said he'd manage. The bellman said he thought the small man had a gun but couldn't verify it. I asked Angelo what room they went to. He told me. I called Lynn and told her about it. She sighed and said she would be indebted to the mob now.

Lynn, Weber, Deacon and the police team gathered in the lobby as the hotel staff were informed as to the nature of our attack. The hotel manager asked if we could be cautious as to the guests on that floor. The desk clerk said that the persons in the room number that Angelo supplied had checked in about two hours ago and paid with cash for one night. Weber said that sounded good enough and called for a warrant. Everyone piled into the elevators, went up to the fifth floor, and waited down the hall for the warrant. Weber called the DA again, asked where the warrant was, and was told the judge was reluctant to give it out. Weber burst out with obscenities and said to fuck him. He led the charge as we went down to the room. Lynn knocked on the door and said "Room Service." There was no answer.

One of the cops found a maid and dragged her to the door. Weber demanded she open it. She was terrified and did so. The police streamed into the room and found Warren tied to a chair. But no Norton.

Bob Moats

As Deacon and Weber were untying him, Warren said that Norton told him he was going out to get something to eat and would be back shortly. Out in the hall a cop yelled for someone to stop, and then there was a gunshot. The cops all piled out of the room and the officer who fired the gun said that Norton was in an elevator when the door opened and he saw him. The rest was heard by all. Norton managed to close the door and went down three flights, then got off, running down the stairs to the ground floor where he vanished into the crowd.

Everyone was pretty happy that we had Warren back, but Norton was still loose. Weber said he'd give any man a month's paid vacation for the head of Norton. Then he said he didn't say that.

Trapper and I went back to the SUV where our weary troops were getting a little crazy from being in the SUV most of the day. I took everyone to a great little Italian restaurant on Flamingo Road, and we ate then went back to the Tropicana. I bought everyone tickets to go see Maria's show, and we relaxed for the night. Maria was glad to see Buck was still in town, and they went off into the night. I told Buck to call in as to when we would go back to Michigan. He said he would.

Trapper and Becker said they were going to hit the strip and see what trouble they could get into. Penny, Willy and I went up to our room to crash for the night. We went up the elevator and when the door opened on our floor we got out and went down towards our room. I didn't pay much attention to the secondary elevator door which opened a minute later or the person who came out and went down the hall. I reached in my pants pocket for the room key card and as I found it I looked over and saw the man. He was pointing a gun at us; it was Norton.

"Didn't think I knew who you were, eh, Richards? I managed to get Warren to talk about a number of things by threatening to kill his cop friends. I found out about your interference with my attack on the bitches of the earth. You just don't know the horror of it all, do you, with your new bride here, Penny Wickens? I used to watch your show. Pretty good if I say so myself. Too bad you won't be able to talk about my story. Or maybe I'll use the two of you to get what I want. My new hostages. I think you are a bit more valuable than a cop." He told us to get into our room and sit. Penny pushed Willy back into his bag, zipped it up and set the doggy purse on the floor next to the couch, hoping Willy would go to sleep.

"I followed you after I saw you and your friends leave the Excalibur and come to this hotel. I waited patiently for you to get finished at the show here, watched which floor your elevator stopped at and came up." He threw me a couple of plastic wire ties and told me to secure Penny. I did and then he told me to get comfortable while he plotted his next move.

I had to stall for time. "I have to say you had the cops going for a while when you were killing off the Bridezillas. Too bad you had to put it on the Internet. That was your downfall. Vanity can be a deadly foe."

He turned and snarled at me. "Bridezillas are evil. They are the deadly foe, and I wanted the world to know of my accomplishments. I was going to list them as I eliminated them, but you had to stick your nose in it, had to snoop around in my web files. If I knew it was that easy, I wouldn't have put the list on the server for you to read. Oh, well, I will have fun now making my new demands with the famous Penny Wickens as my hostage and a recent bride." He went to Penny and asked, "Are you a Bridezilla, Penny?" He looked at me. "Is she a Bridezilla?"

"No, Penny is one of the good brides you spoke of on your website, the kind of bride you were trying to separate from the Bridezillas. Tell me, Harry—may I call you Harry?—you changed weapons for the first few kills, why?" I was trying to distract him from Penny and figured his vanity would get to him.

"I wanted to change the rules a bit, mess with the cops' heads, make them wonder and distract them from who I may have been."

"Zora must have really hurt you," I said.

He exploded. "Don't mention that bitch's name to me. She's dead to me along with all the other bitches that ripped their men's hearts out and crushed them."

My cell phone rang. I just sat and looked at Norton. "If I don't answer it, they may come to see me. You don't want guests, do you?"

Chapter 30

He stood for a minute, thinking, then said to answer but "tell them you're tired and don't want anyone coming by." He waved his gun around Penny's face and said to be careful what I said.

I answered the phone, noting that the caller ID said it was Trapper.

"Hey, Willy Boy, what's happening?" I answered.

I heard a gurgle on the other end. "I told you never to call me that, didn't I?"

"Yeah, Willy Boy, we're settled in our room ready to hit the sheets. We're tired and don't need to party tonight. So you and Weber can go out drinking by yourselves and I'll see you in the morning."

There was a silence on the other end, and then I heard him say, "Trouble in paradise?"

"Yeah, Willy, we'll talk later. Take care and good-bye." I hung up. Trapper once told me that he never said good-bye because it was associated with the death of a couple of loved ones in his past, and that he hated the name Willy boy. I figured he was smart enough to figure it out.

I quickly changed the subject. "So what are you going to do about Zora, kill her, too?"

He grinned. "Yeah, I got her lined up for the kill when I get back to Jackson. Everyone in Mississippi will welcome me with open arms for my accomplishments of bringing better harmony to the sacred wedding bliss. I will take her to the altar of sacrifice and offer her up as an example for men everywhere to eliminate the scourge of the earth, evil women."

This guy was a nut job. "Do you think you can rid the earth of all the evil women? That's a lot of work."

"Oh, I won't have to do that daunting task. Men everywhere will take up my cause. It will spread exponentially, and the wave of retaliation will spread across the face of this globe, and we shall be at harmony."

My cell rang again. I looked at him and said they'd be coming if I didn't answer. He looked annoyed, said to get it done and held the gun to Penny's head.

It was Lynn. I answered, "Hello."

"Are you in trouble? Trapper called me."

"Yeah, we're going back to Michigan tomorrow. Are you coming to see us off?"

"Stall for time. We're on our way, about ten minutes. Trapper is in the hotel. I told him not to be brave." She hung up.

"We'll be glad to see you. Take care." I hung up. I winked at Penny; she got my message.

"So, Harry, why the helicopter to Mexico? That's a long way from Mississippi."

"Come on, Richards, you're supposed to be a smart P.I. At least that's what Warren told me. I was just messing with the cops again. I wasn't going to take a helicopter ride anywhere. While all the cops were standing around with their heads up their asses at the helicopter center, I was going to be on my way out of town, maybe start my Bridezilla franchise in another state till I worked my way back to Jackson." He was grinning widely and pacing around the room waving the gun. I hoped he didn't accidentally shoot it.

Bob Moats

Someone knocked at the door. Norton looked panicked and went to the peep hole. He saw a woman with a cart of what looked like food. He returned to me and said to get rid of them. I looked at Penny and hoped she knew enough to drop if there was gunplay. I went to the door, opened it a crack, and peeked out. The woman said "Room service," and I said we hadn't ordered it. She looked to her right, then left and ran away. I saw the huge shadow that was Angelo moving over to the door. He grinned at me, and then I saw three men behind him, all wise guys. Trapper popped up next to them and I stepped back and said to Norton, "It looks like a good meal. You hungry?"

He came over to the door, and when he got there, I opened it wide. He froze as he saw the men all holding big guns on him. Trapper dove at him low as the rest of the men piled on, grabbing his weapon and holding on to his arms and legs. I thought they were going to play make a wish with him, holding him up in the air, but they just held on to him as he screamed and squirmed.

I walked over, smacked his cheeks a couple of times and said to be nice. I went to Penny, took out my pocketknife and cut the straps binding her hands. She jumped up and hugged me. Then she went to let Willy out of his bag as I went back to the men who were holding Norton upright.

Bridezilla Murders

"You want we should take him out to the desert, Mr. Richards?" Angelo grinned as Norton looked terrified. Trapper, holding his gun on Norton, looked at me and said, "It would save taxpayers a lot of time and money." He winked at me.

"No, thank you, Angelo. The law needs to work him over now," I replied to his kind offer.

"Oh, yeah, he did kidnap a cop, didn't he?" Angelo said. I took the strapping out of Norton's pocket and bound his arms and legs. Norton was still bitching about everything—the straps were too tight, he was being handled too harshly, he was being held against his will. Finally I had enough and cold cocked him right off his feet.

Lynn and Deacon came around the corner of the door and saw the knock down. She looked at the hulking men standing around and said, "I don't want to know."

An army of cops came in and carried Norton out. Lynn and Deacon were introduced to Angelo and his "boys," and Trapper sat on the couch smiling like a Cheshire cat.

I went over to Trapper and asked how he knew to find Angelo. He said, "When I watched you call Angelo the last time, I noted the phone number. I called him and said you were in danger, and he came running with a couple of his men. We plotted the room service thing and got to your door hoping you wouldn't screw our plan up."

Lynn came over and said that Trapper was just as bad as me, just wouldn't listen. She thanked us both and said she was glad Penny and I weren't hurt. I said to be more careful with Norton, that he wasn't totally stupid. She said she would have a whole lot of police on him now.

Everyone had left our suite, and I took Penny's hand and pulled her to the couch. "I guess this puts an end to our little vacation honeymoon. Exciting, wasn't it?"

She smiled and said she wouldn't have it any other way. Willy jumped up and tried to lick both of us; we let him.

Next morning I was doing some last minute errands when Lynn and Deacon came by to see if we needed help to get to the airport. I said I had a few things to do, but they could go round up Buck and Maria and come back in about two hours. They went off. I took Penny to our SUV and we went over to the Excalibur and up to the room I was told was Angelo's. He opened the door, gave us a big smile and asked us to come in. We did. He said to sit, but I said we were getting ready to head out of town and back to Michigan, that we just wanted to stop and thank him for all his help.

"No problem, Mr. Richards. It was a pleasure to be of help."

I held out a small package and said it was a thank you gift from us. His eyes went wide and he took the package, opened it and got a big smile on his face looking at the Rolex watch I got for him. He got all gooey acting and said this was the nicest thing anyone ever did for him. He came over and gave me such a hug I thought I was going to lose my breath. He backed off and said he hoped we would see each other again. Penny and I left him standing at the door waving.

Penny kissed my cheek in the elevator and said that was nice. I asked if she had fun in Vegas, and she said she wouldn't have missed it for the world. I said we would definitely have to come back and rescue Las Vegas from other dastardly criminals again.

Two hours later we had all the baggage at the jet and the SUV returned. Buck and Maria were making moony eyes at each other, and Trapper and Becker were saying good-bye to Deacon and Lynn. Well, Becker was saying good-bye. Trapper didn't.

Lynn said to me that she hoped we were taking all my mob friends with us. I laughed and asked what was her problem with the mob. She smiled and quietly said that her father used to be a mob enforcer in Vegas years ago, that's why she went into law enforcement. We laughed and I gave her a hug. I dragged Buck away from Maria, and we all got on the plane followed by the camera crew, still filming. The door was closed, and we were fastened to our seats and heading up to the blue sky.

Epilog

We reached Michigan safe and sound and went back to our lives. Everyone was thoroughly happy about their week in Vegas and had stories to tell. Weber sent Trapper a big bouquet of black roses with a card saying, "Don't come back," and he promised Becker they would return. Buck went off to get his life in order, thinking more about returning to Vegas to be with Maria. When we got back, I called Lynn and Deacon to let them know Vegas was safe from us now, we were back in Michigan. Lynn said that Norton was under heavy security in solitary. All was good.

One week later, Penny had her show with our video wedding album; I had to admit it was pretty good. She even dragged me to be on the show. We sat and talked about the trip out and our family being there with us. Penny showed photos that my son had been taking of her and the baby, along with the rest of the family. We tried to downplay the murders during our wedding time out there, but did mention it occasionally, saying there was to be another show coming up in a week exclusively about the Bridezilla murders.

Then her show the next week was about the crime in Vegas. It was heavily advertised, and Penny talked me into coming on the show again to give my story. I was secretly thrilled. Willy and I sat as she asked questions of me about our adventures. She had a phone link to Lynn in Vegas and asked her some questions about the case. It was a good show, and we had it on the TiVo.

Three months later, with all the video that the film crew and I had taken of the killer's exploits and the publicity about Norton's TV demands, it was an easy conviction and a quick jury decision. Only took 20 minutes to deliberate. Norton got four counts of life without chance of parole and was whisked to federal detention for the two counts of life for kidnapping. He would never see the sunshine again.

Between the Classmate murders and now the Bridezilla murders, Penny was quite the celebrity, and I sat at my laptop to finish my novel about the classmate murders that I started almost a year ago and abandoned to do my P.I. business. Next, I would start my novel about the Bridezilla killer. I sat at my laptop, thinking that maybe I'd become a writer; it was safer than being shot at.

The End.

For every ending there's a new beginning.

~~*~~

Preview from Sixth Book, "Magic Murders"

Chapter 1

I finally got around to putting a nice 42-inch LCD widescreen TV in my office, right across from the couch, to while away the boring days of waiting for a client to walk in the door. Maybe I should advertise a bit harder. I could also watch Penny's show now while I whiled away the day. That way I could also admire my new bride, as she did her best to smile while trying to munch on a zucchini slice covered in tofu cream. Yum.

The reason she was forcing the zucchini slice was due to a health nutritionist on today's program, showing people how to make healthier meals out of things like squash. Eeuw. I'd rather eat dirt, more roughage. Penny was trying not to make faces at some of the other rather unappetizing delights that the woman presented. I knew Penny's faces well enough now to recognize when she didn't like something. I was also worried that Penny would bring home some of those unappetizing meals to pawn off on me. With the TV, I now had an idea of what to expect when I got home.

It had been about four months since Penny and I were married in Las Vegas and had made it through the Bridezilla murders, now things were pretty much back to normal for everyone. Trapper and Becker were back to fighting crime in Clinton Township; Buck was still mooning about moving back to Vegas and living with Deacon's sister, Maria. I was just waiting for him to fly the coup. My family survived the trip and were all back to their normal routines. My mother had a bunch of pleasant memories and a copy of the wedding video from Penny's show. She enjoyed seeing herself on television.

Deacon and Lynn kept us informed as to how things were doing back in Vegas since we had left, crime, they said, was down twenty percent. I think that was a stab at us.

My office door flew open and in walked an old face I hadn't seen in years. Old face as in age, he was looking worse in years than I did.

"Marty, how the hell are ya?" I asked, standing and coming around my desk to shake his hand. The idiot he was, had a joy buzzer in his hand, startling me. "You dumb ass, haven't changed have you. Despite looking like they just dug you up, you still are a child."

Marty gave me a big grin, then asked if I had a bit of libation. I said I had no alcohol in the office, I was a beer drinker, but not during office hours. He looked disappointed and sat in my client chair as I sat back in my squeaky chair.

"Jimmy, as much as I hoped you wouldn't, you look good for your age. How do you do it?" Marty laughed with a wheeze and a cough.

"Clean living and lots of sex." I said, with a smirk.

"Hell, you wouldn't know what to do in bed with a real woman." He laughed.

I leaned forward and turned the picture of Penny that I kept on my desk and said, "I just married this woman who shares my bed, she keeps me young."

He pulled out a pair of narrow glasses and moved his head closer to the picture, "Crissake, man, that's the woman from the TV isn't it?"

"Yep, Penny Wickens-Richards now. You still single?" I smiled.

"Hell, I haven't found the woman that can put up with me." He laughed.

"Still performing?" I asked, knowing Marty was another magician from way back when he and I used to do shows locally.

"Yeah, I still work the damn kid shows and the occasional adult party, but times are tough and the damn kid magicians are undercutting my standard fees. They aren't worth a crap, but the people will pay their fees rather than go for experience and class." He looked disturbed, as if he had a pain in his stomach.

"You all right Marty?" I asked, concerned.

"Hell, no. I'm all eaten up inside, too much partying and drinking. I'll be lucky to reach my next birthday. But I don't care, my life has been full and I'll go to my coffin with a bottle tucked under my arm. Nobody wants an old fart magician who can't stand doing kid shows any more." He smiled but it was a sad smile.

"What brings you here to my humble office, Marty?"

"I heard you got into the P.I. business, I need a favor." He paused as if his mind drifted to places unknown.

I waited then said, "What is it, Marty?"

"Huhn? Oh yeah, I have been asked to be the recipient of a lifetime award for my service to the

220

world of prestidigitation. You're a magician from way back, I even remember your little magic store you had in Roseville. I want to know if I can hire you to see that I get to the ceremony safely. I'm old and I may lose my way there, or forget all about it." He smiled at me then gave me a toothy grin.

"Marty, how old are you?" I wondered.

"I'll be seventy-four in September. Old enough to know better, but my body says I'm about ninety-nine."

I never had asked Marty his age before, I just assumed he was a bit older, now it hit me to know just how old he was. I'll be 61, a couple months away, if I didn't get shot first.

"Where are you receiving this prestigious award at?" I asked.

"Right here in Michigan, out in Colon, the Magic Capital of the World, well, was before mass production took over and all magic props are now being made in China. Oughta be a law against it." He smiled again. "They're having the annual magic convention and some idiot decided to honor me with an award before I croak. Damn nice of them to think of me now."

I knew that Marty had more magic in his head than twenty kid magicians combined, he had written a couple books on close-up magic, but his forte was stage. Me, I preferred doing comedy magic and my act was funny if I have to say so, which I just did.

"When is the convention this year?" I asked.

"Next month, early this year, I think they moved it so they don't have to give me the award posthumously. That's why I want you to help me make it out there. Keep me in line and standing upright, even if you have to hold me up." The toothy grin came out again. "How much do you charge for protecting this old body?"

"Marty, I could never charge you, besides you couldn't afford me."

"Hell, I got money, I've stashed it away for over forty years, easy to do when you aren't tied down to a wife. But since you offered, I'll take it."

"I knew you would, you old cheapskate. I remember when we used to work the fairs, you always managed to get me to pay for our food and drink."

"Well, you were making the big bucks, being the hotshot magician you were." He laughed.

"Yeah, and look where it got me. No one is giving me any awards." I said with a touch of remorse.

"That was because you took magic on like a business, just doing the shows, but you never associated with other magicians, except me."

"I never liked most of the other magicians; they all thought they could actually walk on water. I was disillusioned that I knew how the trick was done, so the magic was taken all out of it. I just enjoyed the laughter of the audience and having fun with them, not trying to make them think I could actually do magic. You've seen my act, I don't pretend to be a wizard. Too damn many Harry Potters out there."

"Too easy going you were, young Luke." He made the comment sounding like Yoda. And he looked like him. "Jimmy you could have been a legend too, if you chummed up to the right people. You could have been a star."

"Hey, I've performed in Las Vegas, I'll have you know. Lots of shows and I was well received."

His eyes widen, "You actually made it to Lost Wages and worked the stages?"

"Well, not exactly the big stages, a bunch of small ones in the casino malls, hawking magic tricks to the tourists." I said with a sly smile.

"Ah, still the business man, not the magic man." He stood, "I have to be going, business and a bottle to attend to, I'll call you with the details, and Jimmy...

it's good to see you again." He turned to the door and went out.

I sat quietly for a long time, remembering my days doing shows at clubs, bars, fairs, private parties, and even a couple of times on television. OK, I was on the Bozo the Clown show doing magic twice but it was TV. My magic store was a great place to meet people, but after a while the people I met were just all a bit off the wall. Some where nice, most were wrapped up in their magic. I would join a few in a bar and all they wanted to do was talk magic and outdo each other with some new trick they learned. I just wanted to enjoy the evening drinking with a few friends. After a while I stopped going out with them, they just drained the life out of me. I loved performing for an intimate crowd, like in a small bar. I had one place in Mt. Clemens that I performed every Friday and Saturday nights. I was there for almost a year, having fun with the customers. My act was the same every night, but they would bring in friends for me to call up on stage and have fun with them, not embarrassing them but having fun. Those were good days.

Unfortunately, I knew I could never go back.

*

Continued in book...

Bob Moats

Jim Richards Family of Readers

Thanks to the following people who are now part of the Jim Richards Family of Readers. They have read a book or more and enjoyed them. They all volunteered to be included in the list. If you are a fan of the books, send me your full name and you will be included in future books. Send your name to murdernovels@bobmoats.com to be added here and on the website. (updated 03-26-14)

* Achim Feifel * Al Norris * Alex Wheatley * Alexandra Delporte-Wilkinson * Amy Tapia * Andrea Bryan * Anne Shepherd * Arianda Sugar * Arlene Markowski * Ashley Augustus * Audra Hall * Barbara Hughes * Barbara Sammons * Barbara Schuler * Barbara Zirger * Beth Donohue Plenskofski * Betsy Childress * Beth Gibson * Bill Sandy * Bill Tornquist * Billie-jo Collie * Boni J Rychener * Carl Bishopric * Carla Lewis * Carole Henderson * Carolyn Conroy * Carolyn Riddle-Linington * Cassy Bailey * Chad Hudson * Charlotte L Duran * Cheryl L. Everett * Cindy Ackley Nunn * Cindy Valstad * Connie Bancroft * Corinne Kay O'Daniel * Dana Robbins Chuchran * Dana Wichita * Danielle Monique * Darren Heald * Dave Travers * David Wilkinson * Dawn Carpmail * DeAnn Jannereth * Deanna Miller * Deb Breuker Balbo * Debbie Carter * Debbie White * Deborah Fartuch * Deborah Gauze * Deborah Sullivan * Dee King * Denise Freeman * Diana Carver * Dixie Beck * Donna Gould * Donna Thompson * Donny Minter * Doris Kight * Eddie Moore * Eric Walters * Felicia Annette Bradfield * Francine Menor * Gail Chesney * Georgiann Minster * George Conner * Greg Colucci * Hayley Rankin *

Bridezilla Murders

Harold Garcia * Heidi Arnold * Irma Ranee Coy * Jacqueline Moss * Jan Kimball * Janice Schneider * Janice Spoor * Jennifer Redmond * Jessica Keown-Belous * Jim Beck * Jo Boguslaw * Jo Turner * Joanne Marie Turner * John Peiffer * John Wisbiski * Joseph Wauro * Joyce Stacy * Joyce Trifiletti * Judy Franklin * Judy Travers * Judy Padgett * Julie Heath * Junnahvee Benson * Karen Dahl * Karen Grams * Karen Higham * Karen Kaiser * Karen Meinburg Richwine * Karen Kirkman Parker * Karin Hawkins * Karin Vasvari * Kathleen Donohue Roesing * Kathleen Riddle-Wolfe * Kathy Hinds Moore * Kathy Jones * Kathy Mitchell * Katie Benzler * Kay Burns * Kelly Garcia * Ken Boggs * Keota Rodriguez * Kiera Mccarthy * Kim Estes * Kitty Stolle * Kristie Sciler * Kirsty Stanton * LaLonnie Scallen * Larry Morris * Leann Parr * Lenora Scales * Leslie Marie Jackson * Linda Forester * Linda Ingle Cox * Linda Kennerö * Linda Magill * Lisa Bower * Liz Gibson * Lorraine Wiman * Loretta Alexander * Lynda Bowles * Lynette Lawrance * LuAnn Louttit * Manny Rothman * Marcia Gibson DeWitt * Marie Calder * Marlene Bryan * MaryLouise Kramp * Mary Lynn Gross * Megan Atkins * Meghan Hyden * Melody Cannavan * Michael Carruthers * Michael Dinkens * Michael Vannoy * Michelle Burns-Mitchell * Michelle Pilcher * Micki Potter * Mike Moats * Mimi Baur * Myrna Hecht * Nadine Sutton * Natalie Quine * Neena Martin * O'Della Wilson * Pat Pollington * Pat Rohn * Patricia Jarmon * Patricia C Trezza * Patrick Barry * Paul Lawrance * Peggy Davis * Phyllis Bassett * Raylene Matheny * Rebecca Collins Besner * Renee Brumley * Reta Hanna * Reta Moats * Roberta Navarro-Harder * Sally Berneathy * Sally Hubler * Sarah Santos * Satka Nikc * Sharon E. Edwards * Sharon Mangini * Sharon McMillon * Sheena Rawl * Sherry Amstutz * Shirley Alvarez * Shirley Davies * Shirley Williams * Stacie Rowe * Stephanie Conner * Steve Cullen * Susan Haughton * Susan Hesse Adams * Susan Salomon * Suzan K Chase *

Bob Moats

Taisha Cullum * Tamara Moore * Tammy Castleberry * Tammy Lynn Wood * Ted Murphy * Terri Atkins * Terri Creech * Terry Raab * Tonia Rachael Riggs-Williams * Travis Fleury-Lopez * Twyla Gawlas * Val Brooks * Walt Munsel * Yvonne Isakson *

Thank you to all these wonderful people.

Thank you for purchasing this book. I hope you enjoy it as much as I enjoyed writing it for my faithful readers. Please feel free to email me to tell me what you thought about my stories. I love hearing from the readers. I can be reached at murdernovels@bobmoats.com thanks again!

www.ingramcontent.com/pod-product-compliance
Lightning Source LLC
Chambersburg PA
CBHW070624130626
46556CB00001B/458